THE MERMAID CHRONICLES

MARISA NOELLE

For the ones with seashells in their pockets
and dreams of mermaids in their hearts,
may this book cast a spell that lingers like
the scent of salt in the air.

Table of Contents

PART ONE

MERFOLK HISTORY

In the Beginning

In the age before time, when the cosmos were nothing but a blank canvas, there existed three gods of water; Vorago, his sister Cascadia, and his brother Tempest. They were creatures of the deep, born from the ethereal embrace of water and fire, and their purpose was to shape the world we know today. The gods of water, powerful and ancient, resided in the deepest abyss of the ocean. Together, they held dominion over the vast expanse of the watery realm and dreamed of creating something extraordinary beyond their aquatic domain.

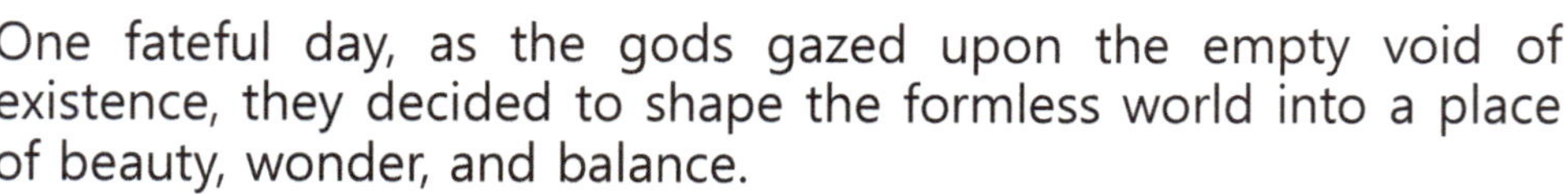

One fateful day, as the gods gazed upon the empty void of existence, they decided to shape the formless world into a place of beauty, wonder, and balance.

Vorago, in the form of a mighty sea serpent, plunged into the abyss. With a single flick of its tail, he summoned forth great tidal waves that carved out valleys and mountains, molding the land into a tapestry of enchanting landscapes. Each crest and trough, each ripple and whirlpool, bore the mark of their divine touch.

The second god, Cascadia, transformed into a graceful dolphin and swam through the newly formed seas. Her laughter echoed across the waters as she birthed rivers, lakes, and ponds, imbuing them with the spirit of life. The creatures that emerged from her joyous play became the first inhabitants of this emerging world.

The third god, Tempest, took on the form of a colossal whale and dived to the depths of the ocean. With a deep, resonant song, he called upon the minerals and treasures hidden within the earth. From the caverns of the deep, he unearthed jewels, metals, and crystals, adorning the world with dazzling beauty.

Next the gods created life in the image of themselves; the ocean shapeshifters were beings of unparalleled grace, with the ability to

transform into any creature of the sea at will. They possessed scales that shimmered like the moonlight dancing on waves and eyes that held the wisdom of the ages. They rose from the depths of the ocean and ascended to the surface, where they encountered a beautiful, newly formed world. As the gods continued their work, the ocean shifters observed in awe and approval. Vorago and Cascadia's love flowed through the world, ensuring that the seas and rivers teemed with life, while their gentle embrace kept the land in perfect harmony.

With time, the world blossomed into a realm of boundless wonder, a reflection of the gods' dreams and their efforts. The oceans sparkled with countless hues, the land flourished with lush forests, towering mountains, and fertile plains, and the skies were painted with vibrant sunsets and shimmering auroras.

In the end, the gods of water bestowed upon their children a final gift—the ability to return to their true forms as ethereal beings, guardians of the seas and the world they had crafted. The ocean shapeshifters became the protectors of nature and the keepers of ancient stories.

History of Ocean Shifters & Atlantis

Long ago, in the age of myths and legends, the merfolk and the selachii thrived beneath the waves. Their world was a paradise, teeming with vibrant coral gardens, luminescent creatures, and the enchanting music of the ocean's currents. Among these marine beings, there was a profound reverence for their benevolent ruler, Vorago, the god of the sea.

It is well documented that first life took place in the water. Merpeople evolved several centuries before humans, and to begin with were confined to the world's oceans. Knowing no different, the merpeople were content with their vast watery world.

Merpeople were originally gifted with beautiful singing voices, and their fascination with the human world made them curious and bold. They swam close to sailors, sang to them, and often lured them into the water, unintentionally causing the deaths of those who could not swim. And often giving opportunities for any number of ancient creatures to feed on this newer source of nutrition.

With the development of humans and the ability to walk, the gods took pity on their favorite species and

granted them the ability to shift into human form and explore land on two legs.

But merpeople were hunted. Merpeople were studied and killed. Humans coveted their iridescent scales, enchanted pearls, and the magic that flowed through their veins. It was a time of turmoil, as the undersea communities struggled to survive, hidden away from the relentless human onslaught. With nowhere to turn, the gods granted them the secret land of Atlantis, an island that would be cloaked from the human world and provide sanctuary to any ocean creature or shifter who needed haven. Merpeople at this time were free to come and go between the veiled Atlantis and the human world by carrying one of the magical keys—a large white pearl—often worn on a chain around their necks.

Vorago, witnessing the suffering of his cherished subjects, was moved to intervene. He saw that the merfolk and selachii were the guardians of the ocean's secrets, the keepers of its balance, and the protectors of its beauty. He decided they deserved a sanctuary of their own, far away from the reach of humanity. It was then that Vorago made a momentous decision—he would gift them the wondrous realm of Atlantis.

To create Atlantis, Vorago harnessed the ancient magic of the seas using his powerful trident, and channeled it into a magnificent and awe-inspiring magical orb, known as the Power of the Sea. This orb radiated a brilliant, otherworldly light and contained the very essence of the ocean's might. It would be

the heart and soul of Atlantis, a source of energy, and a protector of the realm.

With great care and devotion, Vorago placed the Power of the Sea within the heart of Atlantis. The moment it was infused with the orb's energy, the entire city shimmered with an ethereal glow. Coral palaces rose from the seabed, iridescent towers stretched toward the surface, and bioluminescent gardens flourished in abundance. Atlantis was born, a place of unparalleled beauty and wonder.

As a reward for the merfolk and selachii's unwavering loyalty and as a sanctuary from the relentless pursuit of humankind, Vorago granted them the ultimate gift: access to the Fountain of Youth. Within Atlantis, this mystical fountain bestowed eternal youth upon its inhabitants, ensuring their longevity and vitality.

The merfolk and selachii thrived in their newfound home, living in harmony with the ocean's rhythms and nurturing the Power of the Sea that powered their kingdom. Atlantis became a beacon of hope for all undersea creatures, a testament to the enduring bond between them and their benevolent god, Vorago.

Losing Atlantis

For centuries, the merfolk and selachii enjoyed a peaceful existence on the island of Atlantis, hidden away from the prying eyes of humans. The memory of persecution faded, and they grew content, perhaps too content. Some felt it was prudent to build escape tunnels beneath the island that would lead to watery exits in times of threats to the royal family. This vast network of underground tunnels and water channels still exists, in varying degrees of repair. As it was added by ocean shifter activity after the island's creation and not part of the original magic of the island, is unsupported by the Fountain of Youth.

In their tranquility, the ocean shifters became lazy and complacent, forgetting the responsibilities that had once bound them together. Skirmishes erupted among their races, with the merfolk neglecting their duties to safeguard the mystical waters and the selachii failing in their roles as vigilant sentries. The harmony that had once defined their lives dissolved into discord, paving the way for an unforeseen calamity.

The dragon kings, beings of immense power and ambition, seized upon their vulnerability and invaded Atlantis. The once-proud island fell into their grasp, and the ocean shifters were forced to flee for their lives. Merfolk and selachii, once again facing the persecution of the human world, sought refuge where they could, struggling to adapt to a world that had long since forgotten them.

Meanwhile, the dragon kings ruled over Atlantis with an iron grip, driving it to ruin. The sacred island, a testament to shifters' ancient heritage, was now in the hands of those who sought to exploit its riches. The dragon kings reveled in their newfound dominion, while the merfolk and selachii, the rightful inhabitants, languished in the shadows of history.

In this new world, merfolk and selachii found themselves estranged and at odds. The bitter memories of their past conflicts festered, and they became enemies in the human realm, unable to transcend the boundaries that divided them. Their ability to transform into human form, a once-prized gift, was lost when they were cursed by the High Council, and they were irrevocably bound to the ocean.

Yet, amid this chaos and despair, hope endured in the form of two bloodlines—the oldest line of mermaids, the descendants of Samantha Blue

(Cordelia and Dylan), and the royal line of selachii, led by Wade Waters and his family. These chosen few were granted the unique ability to retain their shapeshifting powers, a gift bestowed upon them with a purpose. It was a glimmer of hope, a chance for redemption.

The hope was that Cordelia Blue and Wade Waters, representatives of their respective races, might one day reunite their people. They were entrusted with the responsibility of bridging the divide, to rekindle the unity that had been lost, and to prove their worthiness before the High Council. Their journey was fraught with challenges, but it was a journey that carried the weight of their shared history and the promise of a brighter future.

The legacy of Atlantis and the hope of reunification live on through Cordelia Blue, Wade Waters, and their families, as they strive to heal the wounds of the past and forge a path toward reconciliation and redemption.

N
W E
S
San Diego
Lake Echomere
City
Palace
ATLANTIS

N
W
E
S
City
Maya's House
Gardens
Palace
Shops
School
Upper Courtyard
The Great Hall
Dylan's Bar
Fountain of Youth

Marine Elders: Birth of the High Council

Atlantis was home to a diverse array of beings, but none as remarkable as the ocean shapeshifters. These unique creatures had the ability to transform between various aquatic forms, representing different underwater races. However, with their incredible powers came inevitable disagreements and conflicts that threatened the harmony of Atlantis.

Amidst the turbulent waters of these disputes, a High Council was born. This council consisted of four esteemed members, each representing a significant faction of the ocean shapeshifters. They were entrusted with the responsibility of managing the affairs of Atlantis and finding resolutions to the ongoing conflicts. Their powers and authority were granted by the legendary artifact, the Power of the Sea.

NOTE: For more information on individual members, see SIGNIFICANT FIGURES - HIGH COUNCIL MEMBERS

Zale Sefu's Selachii Birth

Zale Sefu, a young man of imposing stature, stood at a towering six-foot-five-inches with a physique that boasted less than five percent body fat. Despite his remarkable physical attributes, life had always been an unending gauntlet of torment for him. Whether it was the misfortune of residing on the wrong side of the tracks, his inclination for solitude, or his unwavering devotion to protecting his younger sister, he had become a perpetual target for the cruelty of high-school bullies. Each day seemed to dawn with a fresh onslaught of ridicule and aggression, but Zale's spirit remained unbroken.

It was during an ill-fated night, when a wintry chill bit into the bones of California's coastline. Zale, a solitary soul who found solace in the rhythmic bounce of a basketball on the court, was trudging home after yet another grueling practice.

As Zale walked along the desolate beach road, out of the shadows emerged a malevolent group of high-school bullies, emboldened by the cover of darkness. They surrounded him with menacing grins, their cruel intentions evident in their eyes. Their voices taunted him, their jeers slicing through the crisp ocean air.

Inescapably, they herded him onto a weathered pier that jutted out into the vast expanse of the restless sea.

There, on the precipice of despair, they pushed him over the edge, plunging him into the treacherous embrace of the ocean. California, renowned for its sun-kissed beaches and gentle waves, seemed to betray him that night. The currents raged with fury as the rips eagerly awaited their unsuspecting prey.

Zale, who had honed his skills on the basketball court, was no match for the relentless power of the ocean. He struggled against the surging tide, his gasps for breath becoming desperate as the persistent waves threatened to claim him. His death loomed ominously, and it seemed as though his tormentors would finally succeed in their malevolent quest.

But in the midst of the abyss, as darkness began to close in around him, salvation came in a most unexpected form. From the depths, a mysterious figure emerged; a selachii. With a grace that defied comprehension, the selachii drew near to the drowning Zale, encircling him in a protective embrace. In that fleeting moment, as the last vestiges of life clung to him, Zale's world was transformed.

The selachii, with a power that transcended mortal understanding, granted him a new existence. The boundaries of his physical form blurred and shifted, and he emerged from the depths not as a man but as one of the ocean's own. A selachii, with a tail that beat more powerfully than his heart, he was reborn into a world where the laws of humanity no longer held sway.

Zale, with newfound purpose coursing through his veins, clung to the hope that the ocean had bestowed upon him. He realized that he had been granted a second chance at life, an opportunity to rewrite the destiny that had been so cruelly scripted for him. Though he could no longer confront his bullies on the shores of humanity, he vowed never to allow anyone to treat him that way again.

With unwavering determination, he resolved to become a leader in this mystical realm beneath the waves, no matter the challenges that lay ahead. The ocean had remade him, and he would, in turn, reshape his own destiny. The saga of Zale Sefu was only just beginning, and the currents of destiny would guide him to places beyond imagination, where merfolk and humans alike would find themselves terrified by the legend of the ocean shapeshifter.

Kraken's Embrace: Depths of the Shifting Tides

The ocean churned with anticipation as the sun dipped below the horizon, casting a fiery red glow across the sea. A battle of mythical proportions was about to unfold, and the fate of the underwater realm hung in the balance. The merfolk, led by their fearless leader Esmerelda, had gathered a coalition of their own kind, as well as formidable allies—the selachii and eelusionists, to face a colossal threat that had risen from the abyss.

In the heart of the tempestuous maelstrom, the monstrous kraken, a creature of legend and dread, reared its colossal head from the depths. Its massive tentacles writhed and thrashed, creating a vortex that threatened to devour everything in its path. The merfolk and their shapeshifter allies, each adorned in armor forged from the shells of ancient sea creatures, circled the behemoth, determination burning in their eyes.

Esmerelda, resplendent in her battle attire, her silver hair shimmering like a cascade of underwater gems, raised her spear high. Her voice, carrying through the water like a melodious hymn, rang out, "To arms, my kin and allies! Today, we defend our sacred home, the realm of the deep! The kraken shall know the might of those who call the ocean their home!"

The battle commenced as the merfolk and shapeshifters, in perfect synchrony, launched their first assault. The selachii, their forms shifting seamlessly from humanoid to razor-toothed predator, surged forward with lightning speed, their jaws snapping shut on kraken's serpentine appendages. The eelusionists, their bodies sinuous and electrifying, wriggled into the kraken's tentacle crevices, delivering powerful shocks.

Meanwhile, the merfolk, using the Power of the Sea, summoned torrents of currents and tides to disorient the kraken, forcing it to retreat momentarily. Esmerelda herself danced gracefully around the kraken's colossal form, her spear carving through the water with precision. With each strike, she called upon the ancient magic of the sea to wound the monstrous creature.

The kraken roared in agony, its ink-black blood swirling in the water, a testament to the ferocity of the merfolk and their shapeshifter allies. But the battle was far from over. The kraken, a creature of primeval power, unleashed a torrent of darkness and despair, attempting to ensnare the minds of its opponents.

However, the merfolk's indomitable spirit and their bond with the ocean proved stronger. Esmerelda's voice rang out once more, this time imbued with the power of hope and unity, breaking the kraken's grip on their minds. The merfolk and their allies redoubled their efforts, their resolve unwavering.

As the battle raged on, the kraken's strength waned. With a final, decisive blow from Esmerelda, the sea erupted in a dazzling display of light and energy. The kraken's massive form crumbled into lifeless fragments, dissolving into the depths from whence it came.

The victorious merfolk and their shapeshifter allies swam amidst the remnants of the vanquished kraken, the ocean once again serene and tranquil. Esmerelda, her spear glowing with the essence of victory, addressed her comrades, "Today, we proved that the might of unity and the depths of our courage can conquer even the greatest of terrors. The ocean remains our home, and we shall forever defend it against all who threaten its majesty."

With that, the merfolk, the selachii and eelusionists, and their indomitable leader rejoiced in their hard-fought victory, knowing that their bond was unbreakable and their realm secure once more.

Whispers of the Deep: The Hound's Awakening

As merfolk gathered in a clandestine council beneath the waves, a sense of foreboding hung in the salty sea breeze as whispers of an impending threat filled their home.

Merfolk, adorned in shimmering scales and wielding tridents and coral spears, huddled together. Their leader, Nautica, addressed her subjects. "Tonight, my brethren, we face a perilous foe," she declared. "Two sea witches, harboring dark powers, threaten our realm. We must defend our home and our future."

The merfolk had heard tales of Aquaria and her sinister counterpart, Serpentina, for years. Legends spoke of their wicked deeds, but tonight, the legends would become reality. The merfolk knew their existence depended on victory.

As the merfolk prepared for battle, a young mermaid named Nerida was entrusted with a sacred task. In her arms, she cradled a human baby, its innocent eyes wide with wonder. It was foretold that this child, born of the land above, would become the oracle of the merfolk, bridging the worlds of land and sea.

The sea witches, Aquaria and Serpentina, arrived with a deafening roar of thunderclouds gathering beneath the waves. Aquaria, with her terrible black eyes and wriggling serpent hair, chanted incantations in a guttural language that sent shivers through the ocean's depths. Serpentina, her inky-black tentacles snaking through the water, joined her in the dark ritual.

Together, their power summoned the Hound of the Ocean, a monstrous sea beast with scales as black as the abyss and fangs dripping with venom. Its poisonous breath left trails of noxious fumes in its wake.

The merfolk lined up in formation, their tridents and spears glinting with resolve, to confront this terrible threat. Nautica led the charge, her trident striking the water with a resounding boom.

A furious battle ensued beneath the waves, as the sea witches and the Hound of the Ocean clashed with the merfolk. Aquaria's magic sent torrents of water crashing down, but the merfolk countered with their own might and determination.

Nerida, the young mermaid protector of the human baby, swam with grace and determination. She used her voice, gifted with the power of song, to soothe the infant and shield it from harm. Her melodic tunes resonated through the water, serving as a beacon of hope for her comrades.

Nautica and her warriors fought valiantly, pushing back the sea witches and their monstrous evocation. The Hound of the Ocean roared in fury, but the merfolk's determination was unshakable.

The battle raged on for what felt like an eternity, a tumultuous dance between light and darkness beneath the unforgiving waves. Finally, with a concerted effort, the merfolk overcame the Hound of the Ocean and subdued the sea witches, their dark powers quelled.

As the sun's rays pierced through the now calm surface of the ocean, Nautica and her fellow merfolk held their heads high, victorious. The baby, held within Nerida's embrace, cooed softly, her innocent laughter echoing through the depths.

From that day forth, the infant grew into the Oracle of the Merfolk, guiding her people with visions of harmony and balance.

The Tragic Human Death of Dylan Blue

A grave threat loomed over the venerable lineage of the Blue family. The tranquility of the merfolk world was shattered when a treacherous selachii named Zale, harboring a deep-seated grudge against humanity, sought to claim dominion over all oceanic shapeshifters. His vendetta led him to the enchanted pearl, a mystical conduit to the esteemed High Council, the arbiters of fate for ocean shifters. Believing that only one shifter race could wield its power, he set his sights on eradicating the merfolk, especially targeting the prominent Blue family.

Zale's chance for revenge surfaced on a sunny October day when the Blues sailed their vessel, The Big Blue. With calculated malevolence, he conjured waves that capsized their boat, leaving Dylan and Samantha Blue vulnerable to his ruthless assault. Zale, in his quest for power, sank his teeth into Samantha, a warning that coerced her into cooperation, for she possessed the knowledge he sought—the secrets of the pearl and the path to Atlantis.

Focusing his brutality on young Dylan, Zale dragged the unsuspecting boy to the ocean depths, intending to use him as leverage over Samantha. However, fate intervened in the form of valiant merfolk armed with spears. They bravely confronted the vengeful selachii, managing to pry Dylan from his clutches. Although he was knocking on Death's door, the merfolk managed to save Dylan by advancing his transformation into a merman through a resuscitation ritual. In the chaos, Samantha's whereabouts became unknown, and Cordelia, along with her father, wisely sought refuge, leaving Zale defeated and wounded.

Bitter and thwarted, Zale retreated, nursing his wounds and biding his time, his insatiable thirst for power undeterred.

Samantha Blue's Refuge: Atlantis Unveiled

When Samantha Blue found herself entangled beneath the waves with Zale, she was in possession of the fabled keys to Atlantis. These keys, entrusted to Samantha, held the power to transport a single soul to the mythical realm.

Meeting Zale underwater that fateful day, she refused to relinquish the keys to him, and so did the only thing she could do, left her family to travel to Atlantis and stop the keys falling into nefarious hands. When she activated the magical gems, she found herself in a desolate Atlantis, marred by decay and chaos. The once-glorious island was now submerged and polluted, its majestic structures in ruins, the fountain broken and bubbling with musty odors. She dragged herself across the shattered courtyard and took the last healing sip the fountain was capable of producing, curing the injures Zale had inflicted.

Amidst the ruins, she discovered a new threat: dragon kings, fearsome creatures whose fiery breath razed the remnants of Atlantis. These creatures, contrary to her expectations, ruled the island with tyranny, their draconian power undeniable. She'd never met a dragon king before, but she knew one was rumored to sit on the elusive High Council.

Captured and interrogated, Samantha was imprisoned within the dilapidated palace for six interminable years. The dragon kings, selfish and ruthless, kept her alive but in utter isolation. Amidst her captivity, she clung to the memories of her family, wondering about the fate of her children—Dylan, Cordelia, and Raina. Thankfully the Power of the Sea was safe with the High Council in their blue chamber where the selfish dragon kings couldn't use it to their advantage.

Samantha was fed and watered, just enough to keep her alive, and the dragon kings never spoke to her. She was eventually unchained, but kept locked in the great hall, with only the books lining one wall to keep her company. Without them, her mental

health would have suffered more greatly. Her thoughts remained with her children, their fates a haunting mystery.

Then, one fateful day, a glimmer of hope illuminated her darkened existence. A portal opened in the ocean, and a formidable army of merfolk and selachii emerged, led by a striking young woman with fiery red hair—Cordelia, Samantha's daughter, her mermaid tail finally realized. The prophecy had unfurled, and the brave Cordelia had come to fulfill it, leading a charge that would change the course of merfolk history.

The Cursed Bond: Cordelia & Wade's Mythic Alliance

On Cordelia Blue's eighteenth birthday, a pivotal moment arrived, urging her to confront the tragic memories of her mother and twin brother's demise, or so she had assumed. Her once-promising swimming career was abandoned, and even baths became a distant memory. Encouraged by her steadfast companions, Maya and Trent, Cordelia embarked on a courageous journey to conquer her deepest fears.

A transformative revelation awaited her as she cautiously ventured into the water: Cordelia discovered her true nature—she was a mermaid! To her astonishment, she learned that her long-lost twin, Dylan, was alive but imprisoned in the watery abyss, unable to take human form due to the High Council's curse.

Amidst the bittersweet reunion, an old flame, Wade Waters, re-entered Cordelia's life, rekindling a passionate connection between them. Yet beneath the surface of their renewed romance, suspicions loomed. Cordelia sensed Wade was concealing something significant, and guarding her merfolk heritage strained their relationship.

Dylan entrusted Cordelia with a magical pearl, a vital artifact essential for locating the elusive High Council—the sole beings capable of restoring merfolk's ability to walk.

However, the pursuit of the pearl was not Cordelia's alone. The selachii, shapeshifting shark beings cursed to the ocean, also coveted it, desperate to regain their legs. The two conflicting species raced fervently to unravel the secrets within the pearl.

When the pearl was stolen, Cordelia made a startling discovery— Wade was a selachii, and she assumed it was him who had betrayed her trust. Meanwhile, her dear friend Trent fell victim to a vicious shark attack, transforming him into one of the selachii.

Lost and uncertain about whom to trust, Cordelia sought solace in Maya and this ancient tome "The Mermaid Chronicles," a repository of their history and prophecies. Maya insisted that merfolk and selachii must unite to reclaim their forgotten legacy.

Cordelia unearthed a forgotten chapter of history where merfolk and selachii coexisted harmoniously on the mythical island of Atlantis until the invasion of the dragon kings disrupted their peace.

With unwavering determination, and learning that Wade was not the one who had betrayed her, Cordelia joined forces with him to retrieve the stolen pearl, confronting the selachii leader, Zale, in a breathtaking battle that put Wade's life in danger. Through their combined strength, a formidable alliance of merfolk and selachii emerged victorious, unlocking the secrets of the pearl, and transporting Cordelia and Wade to another dimension where they would face the High Council.

The High Council, comprising representatives from mermaids, selachii, dragon kings, and eelusionists, made a momentous decision—to restore the use of legs to both species. However, this gift came at a price. Cordelia and Wade were entrusted with an extraordinary mission—to find their lost homeland, the legendary Atlantis.

Finding Atlantis: Cordelia and Wade's Oceanic Oath

When mermaids began mysteriously disappearing, stolen away by humans for display or sinister experiments, the hidden realm of mermaids and selachii was unveiled. Cordelia, Wade, and their friends fought valiantly, rescuing one of their own from a science lab. Yet, the global onslaught continued, casting an ever-growing shadow over their existence.

Their mission was clear: unveil the enigma of the lost island of Atlantis—an aquatic sanctuary where all ocean shifters could find refuge. To unlock its secrets, the team embarked on a quest for the fabled, scattered jewels that opened Atlantis' portal. But their journey was fraught with peril.

Beneath the icy depths of Mount Rainier and the treacherous Puget Sound, Cordelia and Wade faced near-death encounters with ice demons. Gal, a formidable dragon king and council member, defied convention to save them. The Power of the Sea surged through them, healing their wounds and bestowing incredible gifts—a Herculean strength for Wade and the untamed power of fire for Cordelia.

Tensions flared as Wade's ex, Stephanie, intruded on the mission, determined to win him back, fueled by his mother's approval. Cordelia grappled with doubt, their bond tested by misunderstandings and painful infidelities, fracturing their once-unbreakable unity.

Maya's life hung by a thread after a harrowing accident, compelling Dylan to transform her into a mermaid. But the toll of their perilous journey didn't end there—Cordelia's father faced certain death in the unfathomable Mariana Trench, only to be transformed into a selachii through a desperate ritual led by Wade.

Amidst near-tragedies and heartaches, Cordelia and Wade rekindled their love, poised to confront those who sought to tear them apart. Armed with the keys to Atlantis, they crossed dimensions into a magical realm. But a harrowing sight awaited them—an island in ruins, guarded by legions of dragon kings. A savage battle ensued, with Cordelia mastering her fiery abilities to vanquish the malevolent force, at the cost of her dear mentor, Gal.

As the Power of the Sea was plunged into the Fountain of Youth, the island blossomed anew. Amidst the rejuvenation, Cordelia made an astonishing discovery—a long-lost captive, her mother, believed dead for almost six years, was alive and well.

In a joyous reunion, Cordelia found her family and a newfound sanctuary where all could walk on land, hidden from prying human eyes. Amidst the serenity, Wade proposed to Cordelia, promising a blissful future, until the pages of this very book started turning once again.

Waves of Accusation: Ocean Shapeshifters' Trial

In the heart of Spain, there lived a baron of great renown. His name was Alejandro de Vargas, and his life was one of opulence and grandeur. However, amidst his riches and power, there was one treasure that he held above all else—his beloved wife, Isabella.

One fateful evening, under the crimson hues of a setting sun, tragedy struck. Isabella ventured into the tempestuous sea, seeking solace in the waves, unaware of the storm that loomed on the horizon. As the tempest unleashed its fury, Isabella found herself ensnared in the treacherous currents, gasping for breath beneath the churning waters.

In times past, the merfolk and the selachii had been the saviors of those who found themselves drowning. They had the power to rescue and resuscitate, their transformation ritual saving the damned and turning them into members of their underwater races. But the world above had grown increasingly perilous when the human world discovered the existence of ocean shapeshifters and attempted to ensnare their underwater cousins. The merfolk, sensing the encroaching darkness of humanity, had retreated to the safety of Atlantis, their ancient island.

Isabella's cries for help went unanswered as the merfolk and selachii were no longer present to come to her aid. The heartbroken Alejandro de Vargas watched from the shore, helpless, as the love of his life was claimed by the unforgiving sea. Grief overcame him, and in his anguish, he cast blame upon the merfolk, believing they had forsaken their sacred duty.

Consumed by anger and sorrow, Alejandro de Vargas, driven to madness by his loss, devised a terrible plan. He possessed knowledge that had long been kept hidden—the knowledge of a devastating power that could bring about the annihilation of the world itself: nuclear weapons.

Under the shroud of darkness, Alejandro de Vargas conspired with a group of like-minded individuals, and together, they hatched a plan to unleash nuclear devastation upon the world. The ancient legends spoke of a cataclysmic event that could be triggered by the misuse of this power, a punishment for humanity's arrogance and disregard for natural order.

Unbeknownst to the merfolk in their sanctuary, malevolent energies swirled and gathered in the world above. The cataclysmic explosion rent the world asunder, claiming the lives of countless humans, Alejandro de Vargas among them.

Upon their return to the human world and the shocking devastation that met their eyes, the merfolk, moved by a profound sense of responsibility, opened their island sanctuary to the remnants of humanity, seeking to atone for their absence. Yet, not all factions of humanity accepted this benevolence. Some harbored a seething resentment, placing blame for the world's dire state squarely on the shoulders of the merfolk, vowing vengeance against every ocean shifter.

Only through the union of three souls; one mermaid, one selachii, and one human, was the power of Atlantis magnified, enabling them to quell the human rebellion. United at last, the races converged in a fearsome confrontation with the Hound of the Ocean, battling to restore the fragile equilibrium of a world forever changed.

Oceanic Uprising: The Hound Strikes Again

In the time that followed the cataclysmic aftermath of a nuclear war in the realm of humans, a great battle unfolded on the shores of San Diego. The rulers of Atlantis, Cordelia Blue and Wade Waters, held council with the wise elders known as the High Council.

Together, they made a fateful decision, one that would forever alter the course of our world. The veiled shroud concealing Atlantis from the human world was lifted, and a sanctuary was extended to their distant kin, the humans, who had borne the brunt of their own world's destruction.

Yet, not all was calm in Atlantis. Suspicion and unease danced among the merfolk like shadows in the deep. Humans, unaccustomed to magical abilities, cast wary glances at Cordelia's mastery of fire and Wade's unparalleled strength. Many blamed the merfolk and ocean shifters for the horrors of the war.

Among these troubled waters, a tempestuous figure emerged. Stephanie, once the beloved of Wade, had not taken kindly to her rejection. Consumed by jealousy and fury, she delved into the forbidden arts, her rage transforming her into a sea witch. Seeking refuge and power, she turned to the only other sea witch in existence, the enigmatic Aquaria.

Aquaria, ancient and formidable, tutored Stephanie in the dark arts, teaching her how to wield her newfound, terrifying powers. Together, they summoned a malevolent entity known as the Hound of the Ocean, a creature bent on the destruction of the merfolk and ocean shifters, with Cordelia and Wade as its primary targets.

Amidst this turmoil, a glimmer of hope emerged. Humans, led by the courageous Babette and her father Rob, joined forces with the ocean shifters. They stood united to protect their shared lands and thwart the nefarious plans of the sea witch and her unholy companion.

In a moment of selflessness, Cordelia entrusted her engagement ring, a source of mystical power, to Babette. With it, the young human was able to conjure a protective force field that shielded many from the hound's poisonous breath. But as the waters ran crimson with the blood of both merfolk and humans, Cordelia and Wade descended into the depths to confront the monstrous beast head-on.

With the ring's power, Wade's formidable strength, and the fiery breath of Blaze—the last of the dragon kings—they waged an epic battle against the Hound of the Ocean. Their resolve was fortified by a small sample of the Power of the Sea, gifted to them by Edward, the last of the elusive eelusionists.

In a tumultuous clash of elements, Cordelia's fire, Wade's might, and the forces of water itself, they triumphed over the hound, banishing it from our realm forever.

After his devastating series of events, Aquaria was killed by her son, Blaze. Yet, Stephanie remained elusive, a dark shadow lurking beneath the waves, a reminder that even in the watery realm of myths and legends, the seeds of jealousy and betrayal can bear treacherous fruit.

Sea Witch's Final Duel

Stephanie Bowers was a mermaid like no other, bearing a unique curse and a heart consumed by jealousy. The people of Atlantis had witnessed her transformation and turmoil to a sea witch.

After the second brutal encounter with the fearsome Hound of the Ocean, Stephanie vanished from our world. Her absence left an eerie emptiness in the hearts of many, and merfolk began to believe she would never return. But for two souls, Cordelia Blue and Wade Waters, dread still clung to the deep recesses of their hearts, for they knew Stephanie's return was just a matter of time.

It was during a grand celebration commemorating a new dawn of peace that Stephanie reappeared. Her presence was undeniable, her hair alive with venomous serpents, hissing and striking at the heart of Atlantis. Chaos unfurled as the serpents wrought havoc, claiming the lives of many before they could seek solace in the healing waters of the Fountain of Youth.

Wade, ever the voice of reason and compassion, approached Stephanie with a plea in his eyes. He sought to show her the error of her jealous ways, the pain and destruction she had caused. But Stephanie, consumed by her own bitterness, refused to be tempted by his words. She threatened to unleash even greater evils upon the peaceful island, her eyes burning with a malevolence that chilled souls.

Amidst the turmoil, another figure stepped forward. Jordan, Wade's cousin, had been entangled in Stephanie's web of romance, only to be used and discarded. Rage surged within as he realized the depth of her deception. With a swift and desperate motion, he thrust a knife through Stephanie's heart.

In that moment, the world held its breath. Stephanie's serpentine hair disappeared into the sand, and her lifeless form sank into the depths of the ocean. She was gone, and Atlantis breathed a collective sigh of relief.

Stephanie's tale serves as a cautionary legend among merfolk, a reminder of the destructive power of jealousy and the darkness it can breed even in the deepest corners of their hearts.

The Legend of the Trident

This tale has been passed down from generation to generation, whispered in the glistening coral caves where merfolk gathered to share stories. It speaks of the trident's creation, an ancient forging

carried out by the skilled hands of Vorago himself and his talented smith. In the heart of Atlantis, the god of the sea had chosen the hottest volcano to craft the three-pronged golden weapon. Each tine was imbued with the power of the ocean, granting its wielder control over the currents that danced through the deep.

But with great power came great responsibility, and Vorago knew his creation could not fall into the wrong hands. So, he entrusted the trident to the seawolves, fierce and loyal creatures who patrolled the depths surrounding Atlantis. These mystical guardians were half-wolf, half-fish, with sharp teeth that could cut through the toughest of armor and keen senses that could detect the approach of intruders.

The merfolk had always lived in harmony with the seawolves, respecting the delicate balance of their underwater kingdom. The merfolk and the seawolves shared a deep bond, forged over millennia of coexistence. Together, they vowed to protect the trident and keep it out of reach of any who would seek to use its power for evil. Long before Atlantis fell to the dragon kings and fearing the complacency of the merfolk and selachii would lead to greed and war, the seawolves disappeared, taking the trident with them.

One fateful day, centuries later, a shadow fell over Atlantis as rumors spread of a megalodon, a colossal and malevolent creature that terrorized the ocean depths. It was said to be impervious to harm, its skin as tough as the strongest corals, and its hunger insatiable. The megalodon's rampage threatened not only the merfolk but the entire underwater world.

Desperation hung in the water, but a glimmer of hope still remained. According to the ancient legends, the trident possessed the power to pierce the megalodon's impenetrable hide and bring an end to its reign of terror. The merfolk knew that the time had come to retrieve the trident and use it for the greater good.

The seawolves, no longer allies of the merfolk, needed to be charmed by an ice flute crafted by someone with an affinity for snow and ice.

At last, after the flute was crafted, one brave merman—Gal Waters—reached the inner sanctum where the trident was wedged within a boulder, gleaming with an otherworldly light. He knew this was his only chance to save their world from the megalodon's terror.

As he emerged from the depths with the trident in hand, he felt a renewed sense of hope. With the seawolves loyal once more, he embarked on a daring mission to confront the megalodon. The fate of their realm hung in the balance, and the power of the lost city's trident would be the last hope against the relentless creature that threatened Atlantis.

With the ancient trident in his possession and the seawolves at his side, this one brave merman faced a battle of epic proportions, one that would determine the destiny of their island and the legends that would be told for generations to come.

Aquatic Anarchy: The Denizens' War on Gal Waters

Gal Waters, son of Cordelia and Wade and the Prince of Atlantis, is best known for discovering Vorago's trident and using it to defeat Zale, a traitorous selachii who had terrorized his family for decades. After his quest, he settled back into life in Atlantis, but remained wary of The Mermaid Chronicles, especially when a new prophecy appeared revealing he would be instrumental in bringing down the Denizens of the Deep—ancient evil water deities who resided in the murky depths. Terrified of losing Una after finally admitting how much he cared for her, Gal attempted to ignore the prophecy until...

PART TWO

REFERENCE

Merfolk

To understand their origin, one must dive deep into the annals of aquatic history, as passed down through generations of their kind.

In the ancient days, the oceans were their cradle and sanctuary. Merfolk believe their existence is entwined with the very essence of the sea itself. They are the guardians of the oceans, and their lineage can be traced back to a time when the world was still forming, and life had yet to flourish on land. It is said that the waters of the primordial sea gave birth to the first merfolk.

Their most unique ability is their shapeshifting prowess. They possess the remarkable talent to seamlessly shift between two distinct forms: the half-fish, half-person hybrid, which is their most iconic appearance and their natural aquatic form, which grants them unmatched agility and grace beneath the waves; the full human image, which allows them to walk upon the land as if they were one of its terrestrial inhabitants; This gift has allowed them to navigate both the ocean's depths and the world above with ease, adapting to their surroundings as needed.

One of the defining characteristics of merfolk is their ethereal singing voices. Their melodies are hauntingly beautiful, and they hold a deep connection to the currents of the ocean. Their songs have the power to soothe the most tempestuous of seas or enrapture the hearts of those who hear them. Music is not just an art form for them; it is a means of expression, communication, and unity among their people, and unfortunately a talent that has diminished with time.

In times of conflict, merfolk are proficient with spears, which they have wielded to protect their underwater realms from threats both natural and supernatural. Their combat techniques have evolved over centuries, and their agility and dexterity in water make them formidable opponents. Yet, they prefer peace and harmony, striving to coexist with the diverse creatures of the sea.

Communication among merfolk is a unique and deeply personal experience. When submerged in water, they utilize telepathy to converse with one another. This form of communication transcends language barriers and allows them to convey emotions, thoughts, and intentions directly, fostering a profound sense of unity and understanding within their communities.

The merfolk, with their shapeshifting abilities, mesmerizing voices, proficiency with spears, and telepathic communication, are a race deeply rooted in the oceans and the mysteries of the deep. Their history is as vast and boundless as the sea itself, and their connection to the waters runs deeper than the ocean's abyss.

Selachii

The selachii are ancient and enigmatic beings who became the guardians of Atlantis, sworn to protect the merfolk and their allies.

Long before Atlantis rose from the ocean's depths, the selachii were feared and misunderstood by all who encountered them. These shapeshifters possessed the remarkable ability to transform into the mightiest predators of the sea—sharks. Their shifting forms were awe-inspiring, their power unmatched. Yet, their existence was shrouded in mystery, as they seldom revealed themselves to the surface world.

The legend tells of a time when Atlantis was newly formed, a city of grandeur beneath the waves. The merfolk, a graceful and wise civilization, inhabited its crystalline palaces, and the eelusionists were their steadfast allies, their kinship born from a shared love of the ocean's secrets.

But danger lurked in the depths. An ancient evil, a monstrous Leviathan of darkness, awakened from its slumber. This creature, with its insatiable hunger and destructive power, threatened to engulf Atlantis and the merfolk in its malevolence.

Desperation gripped the merfolk, for they knew not how to combat this terrible menace. It was then that the selachii, watching from the shadows, felt a stirring within their hearts. They recognized that the balance of their watery world was at stake, and they could no longer remain hidden.

In a moment of profound sacrifice and unity, the selachii revealed themselves to the merfolk and eelusionists. With a pledge of loyalty and the promise to protect their brethren, the selachii agreed to stand as guardians of Atlantis, to face the Leviathan and save their beloved island.

In an epic battle, the selachii, transformed into a fearsome shark army, clashed with the Leviathan. The ocean churned with their fury, and the very sea seemed to quake. It was a battle that tested the boundaries of their strength and determination.

In the end, it was the unity of the merfolk, eelusionists, and the selachii that prevailed. Together, they overcame the Leviathan, casting it back into the abyss from whence it came.

As a token of their gratitude and newfound alliance, the merfolk and eelusionists welcomed the selachii into the heart of Atlantis. From that day forward, the selachii watched over their oceanic brethren, their shapeshifting prowess honed to protect and defend. They became the eternal guardians of Atlantis, safeguarding the merfolk and eelusionists from any threat that dared to challenge the harmony of their undersea realm.

And so, the selachii live on, a testament to the power of unity and sacrifice in the face of darkness, reminding all who dwell beneath the waves that they are bound by a common purpose—to protect the enchanting beauty of their underwater world and preserve the secrets of the deep for generations to come.

Eelusionists

The origins of the electric eel shapeshifters is a story whispered among the merfolk, handed down through generations like a precious pearl of wisdom. In the heart of Atlantis, there once existed a concealed cavern, illuminated by the radiant glow of luminescent algae. Here, the electric eel shapeshifters, known as the eelusionists, thrived.

The eelusionists were enigmatic beings who possessed the rare ability to transform themselves into electric eels at will. This transformation allowed them to harness the power of electricity, making them not only masters of disguise but also formidable protectors of Atlantis. Their shimmering scales sparkled like stars in the darkest depths, and their electrical currents could both light up the abyss and strike fear into the hearts of any who threatened their home. Although their numbers were always small, their power was mighty, and they fought valiantly when threatened.

The harmony between the merfolk, the eelusionists, and the selachii, was built upon mutual respect and understanding. The selachii were the guardians of Atlantis' borders, fiercely protecting the city from any outside threats, while the eelusionists, with their unique abilities, shielded Atlantis from within.

But it was their unity that truly defined Atlantis. The merfolk, with their enchanting songs, bridged the gap between the eelusionists and selachii, forging an unbreakable bond of friendship and cooperation. Together, they ensured the safety and prosperity of their underwater utopia.

In times of celebration, the merfolk's melodies echoed through the coral halls of Atlantis, and the eelusionists lit up the caverns with their radiant displays of electricity. The selachii, with their powerful presence, swam in perfect formation, embodying the city's strength and resilience. Underneath the waves, Atlantis was a realm where the boundaries of possibility were constantly pushed, where different beings coexisted in a delicate balance, each contributing their unique talents to the collective well-being.

But as the world above grew increasingly tumultuous, Atlantis remained a hidden haven of peace, an enchanting realm guarded by merfolk, eelusionists, and selachii, a testament to the beauty of harmony between beings, no matter how different they may be.

Dragon kings

For countless ages, dragon kings roamed the vast ocean depths, existing alongside the timeless merfolk and selachii, their destinies intertwined when they grew jealous of the bounty Atlantis had to offer and wanted it for themselves. Born with wings initially designed for powerful aquatic propulsion, these majestic beings underwent numerous evolutionary cycles that bestowed upon them the extraordinary gift of flight. As they soared through the boundless skies, their wings, once devoted to underwater navigation, became instruments of both terrestrial and aquatic grace.

Inheriting the quintessential traits of dragons, these beings possess the mesmerizing ability to exhale fire, a skill seamlessly wielded in the ocean's depths as well as upon the land. Shifters blessed with the affinity for fire manipulation can manifest in

diverse forms—appearing entirely human, adorned with the majestic wings of dragons, or fully embracing their draconic essence. With these unparalleled powers, the merfolk and selachii could not protect their island and lost Atlantis to the fiery creatures.

The once-thriving population of dragon kings has witnessed a decline in recent years since the battle for Atlantis when many of them were killed, leaving only a scarce few to carry the mantle of their ancient lineage.

Orcana

The orcana were the keepers of a hidden world, residing in the icy embrace of the Antarctic seas, where their existence was a legend even to the most ancient and wise ocean shapeshifters.

Long ago, when the world was young and the oceans were still teeming with undiscovered wonders, the orcana came into being. They were born from the union of ancient ocean magic and the spirit of the orcas. These shapeshifters were unique, bearing skin markings that swirled with the emotions of their hearts. Each mark on their skin told a story, an intricate dance of color and pattern that revealed their feelings to the world.

At first, the orcana were like any other ocean clan, swimming and shifting between their human and orca forms. But as tensions grew in Atlantis between the merfolk, the selachii, and the eelusionists, the orcana, wise beyond their years, foresaw the brewing conflict and chose a different path.

In the heart of the icy Antarctic waters, the orcana built their hidden haven. With their skin markings as a form of communication, they developed a harmonious way of life, far from the political turmoil of Atlantis. Here, they nurtured their ancient traditions, passing down their shapeshifting abilities from generation to generation. Yet, they also knew the world above was oblivious to their existence, and they preferred it that way.

As the centuries passed, the orcana became reclusive, their numbers dwindling with time. Their clans had almost died out, and the knowledge of their existence faded from the collective memory of the ocean shapeshifters.

The legend of the orcana lived on only as a whisper among the ocean shapeshifters, a story of a clan that chose to remain hidden in their world of swirling emotions and icy waters, that is until a nuclear war decimated the human world, and the ashrays had nowhere left to hunt. With orcana numbers quickly decimated by the ghostly rays, they had no choice but to seek the healing waters of the fountain in Atlantis and reveal themselves to their fellow shapeshifters once more.

Equinids

A mysterious species of seahorse shapeshifters, known as equinids, have remained hidden from the eyes of other ocean shapeshifters for centuries. Equinids are reclusive seahorse shapeshifters, who reside in the hidden corners of the ocean, far away from the territories of merfolk, selachii, eelusionists, and orcana. Their ability to change forms, resembling ordinary seahorses, enables them to camouflage seamlessly among their surroundings, making them nearly impossible to detect.

Equinids were once ordinary seahorses living in the mystical Coral Nexus. Through a magical convergence of lunar and tidal energies, these seahorses gained the ability to shapeshift, transforming into the equinids we know today. They have guarded this secret ever since, ensuring their anonymity in the vast ocean world.

Once a year, during the full moon, equinids gather for the Annual Equinid Games. This grand celebration consists of various races and competitions, where equinids showcase their shapeshifting prowess and agility. These games serve as a way for Equinids to come together, strengthen their community bonds, and honor their ancient traditions.

Despite their reclusive nature, a few instances of equinids interacting with other ocean shapeshifters have been documented. These encounters, rare as they are, have led to whispers and legends among merfolk, selachii, eelusionists, and orcana about the elusive race. However, their true nature and the extent of their abilities remain a mystery, leaving other ocean shapeshifters intrigued and fascinated.

The High Council

The High Council, reporting only to the King and Queen of Atlantis, plays one of the largest parts in Atlantean history, and continues to play a fundamental role to this day. With unique power granted to them by the Power of the Sea, they advise and safeguard the island's inhabitants, as well as interpret the prophecies that affect their futures.

These immortal custodians, perpetually numbering four, wielded dominion over the aqueous domain. The inaugural High Council, stewards of a tranquil Atlantis, upheld the sacred duty of safeguarding the island and its inhabitants, while also casting vigilant eyes upon the veiled tapestries of prophecy. Yet, when the island succumbed to the incursion of the dragon kings, the High Council, aflame with righteous fury at the complacency of merfolk and selachii, decreed a fateful curse upon both, condemning them to eternal oceanic existence and forfeiting their shapeshifting prowess, save for the most ancient bloodlines.

As an added penalty the High Council invented the ashrays to torment the selachii during the moon's dominant hours, as they had failed in their duty as custodians and guardians of Atlantis and allowed the dragon kings to destroy the island.

With the submergence of Atlantis into the abyssal depths, the High Council transcribed The Mermaid Chronicles, translating the prophecies presented by the Power of the Sea into a written language only they could interpret, as well as the one true oracle. This tome was entrusted to a lineage of humans, graced with the gift of prophecy, and charged with sounding the clarion call of warning to the remaining ocean shifters.

During the time Atlantis was lost, the High Council fashioned a magical blue chamber, an ageless sanctuary immune to the ravages of time. Yet, the enchantment that enshrouded them within the chamber dared not cross the boundary into the human realm; should they venture forth, the relentless march of age would befall them.

NOTE: Please see Significant Figures for more information on individual members

The Blue Chamber

The blue chamber stands as an eternal enchanted haven, meticulously crafted by the venerable High Council in the wake of Atlantis's demise. It was designed as a refuge, a timeless sanctuary wherein they sought safety, clinging to life's shimmering thread until the day when Atlantis would rise again.

It is in this chamber they safeguarded the Power of the Sea, a mighty blue orb that is the power source of Atlantis and the Fountain of Youth. Fearful that the powerful orb would be stolen by evil entities and wielded for nefarious means, they guarded the source of Atlantean magic in the blue chamber where no one could enter unless they presented a united front and were in possession of one of the keys—a large white pearl.

The blue chamber was dissolved when Atlantis was reclaimed, and the new High Council currently resides on the island.

The Senate

The merfolk senate emerged as a distinguished assembly of four esteemed ocean shifters entrusted with the governance and legislation of Atlantis. Unlike the ethereal and enchanting facets tended to by the High Council, the senate shoulders the weighty responsibilities of formulating governmental policies and laws, serving as the resonant voice of the oceanic populace. Their esteemed gatherings harmonize with the High Council and the regal rulers of Atlantis, converging to deliberate upon the well-being of their kindred ocean shifters.

The Power of the Sea

The most powerful relic within the ocean shifter realm, the water orb is the pinnacle of Vorago's power and aided him in the creation of Atlantis. It is a magical orb that keeps the oceans in balance and powers the Fountain of Youth, as well as the island itself. The Power of the Sea can be inhaled to save an ocean shifter's life, if they are found worthy, and sometimes leaves the individual with an immense ability. The orb has the ability to reveal prophecies to its protectors. It is made from an unknown nebulous material and small parts can be given to brave heroes embarking on quests to carry with them into either the human world or beyond the veil of Atlantis. The orb will immediately regrow to its original size. It is unknown if anything can destroy the Power of the Sea.

The Elemental Orbs

There are six elemental orbs that possess different functions. They resided in Atlantis in the great hall until the dragon kings invaded the island. At that point the High Council hid five of the orbs in the tunnels beneath the island, and used the most powerful orb—The Power of the Sea, representing the element of water—to create a new dimension, known as the blue chamber, where they would be safe from the war and continue to oversee matters between the ocean shifters. The Power of the Sea remained in this chamber under the protection of the High Council while Atlantis was invaded, lost, and then forgotten.

Each orb has a unique connection to an individual Atlantean, an individual the orb chooses itself, and can grant that shifter immense power, or enhance an ability already established. It is only the orbs which can grant powers and abilities to an Atlantean, but there are other tools that may provide temporary abilities when they are being used, such as the trident and the ice flute. The abilities the orbs gift their chosen individual are varied and always tied to the wielder's emotions.

The Orb of Fire and Heat

When the fire orb selects an Atlantean soul to be its bearer, it bestows upon them the coveted gift of untamed flames. As the orb's chosen, an Atlantean individual becomes a living conduit of the elemental fire, their very essence aflame with a mystical intensity. These gifted ones can command torrents of fire with a mere thought, conjuring blazing infernos that dance in harmony with the undulating currents of the ocean and may have dominion over any fire-breathing shifter.

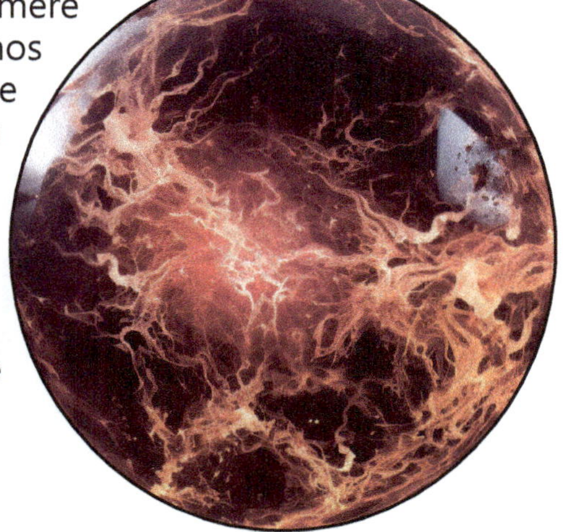

The original guardian of the orb of Fire & Heat was Cordelia Blue. After her tragic death, the responsibility passed to Blaze.

The Orb of Snow and Ice

When this orb chooses an individual, it is as if the very heart of winter resides within their grasp. With a mere thought, they conjure icy tempests that dance through the azure depths, weaving frosty tapestries in the water. The orb's gift allows them to sculpt frozen sculptures of ethereal beauty, turning the sea into a majestic art gallery. Their control over the frigid currents becomes unparalleled, enabling them to freeze adversaries with a mere glance or shield their kin from harm. Under the orb's icy guidance, these chosen Atlanteans become the guardians of our oceanic realms, their powers as awe-inspiring as the icy depths themselves. It is this chosen individual who will be granted with the gift of carving a magical flute from ice and snow.

The current guardian of the orb of Snow & Ice is Gal Waters.

The Orb of Rock and Earth

This orb bestows upon its chosen individual the unparalleled gift of nature's dominion. To the merfolk, these chosen ones become the embodiment of the sea's harmony and earth's resilience, and some consider it to be a more powerful orb than the Power of the Sea, for it only goes to those who are purest of heart and have a perfect balance of love and respect. With the orb's grace, they can harness the earth's energy, sculpting mighty landscapes or quelling the fiercest of quakes. The merfolk watch in awe as the chosen Atlantean is entrusted with the delicate balance of their world, knowing that through this magical connection, the truest essence of nature itself flows through their veins, ensuring the prosperity and preservation of Atlantis for generations to come.

The current guardian of the orb of Earth & Rock is Ford.

The Orb of Air and Flight

The Air & Flight orb has long intrigued the merfolk society. To them, the notion of taking to the skies is as foreign as the realms beyond the ocean's horizon. Yet, they have heard tales passed down through generations about the transformative powers this mystical orb bestows upon chosen Atlantean individuals. It is said that those fortunate souls selected by the orb find themselves blessed with the extraordinary ability to harness the air itself, granting them the power of flight. To merfolk, the thought of soaring high above the water's surface and breathing the air of the world above is a tantalizing dream, forever bound to the realm of fantasy. Nonetheless, we watch with curiosity and wonder as these chosen Atlanteans take to the skies, forever touched by the magic of the Air & Flight Orb. With wings of wind and breaths of cloud, they navigate effortlessly through the boundless heavens, becoming a bridge between the world above and the world below. The merfolk hold deep respect for these aerial guardians, for they understand that the harmony between sea and sky is a reflection of nature's true magic, a balance upheld by the chosen few who possess the Air & Flight Orb's radiant powers.

The current guardian of the orb of Air & Flight is Dylan Blue.

The Orb of Spirit and Soul

When this orb selects an Atlantean individual, it is said that their spirit becomes imbued with the vitality of the oceans, granting them the power to manipulate currents, communicate with the mysterious creatures of the deep, and harness the raw energy of the tides. Yet, it is not just physical prowess that the orbs unlock; they reveal the depths of one's soul, endowing them with the wisdom of ages past and an unbreakable bond with the mystical world below. The Spirit & Soul orb, with its purple aura, grants a profound connection to the very essence of life, and unlocks the depths of emotion and empathy, empowering its bearer to heal the wounds of heart and soul. In the hands of the chosen Atlantean, these orbs become vessels of harmony, fostering unity between land and sea, and embodying the magical tapestry of the Atlantean world.

The current guardian of the orb of Spirit & Soul is Una Summers.

Note about the Orbs

The orbs can be combined to create a great and terrible power, but only if all those who have an affinity with their individual orbs are present. The combined orbs can turn death to life, or life to death, and can only be used once per century as their strength will be vastly depleted. Once they have granted their combined power, they will separate themselves once more and it will take years for their full power to be restored. The chosen individuals will also have significantly reduced powers during this time.

The Magical Keys

The Pair of Rubies

There exists a pair of enchanted rubies known as the Atlantean Gemstones. They were created by the Sea Sorceress, a powerful merfolk mage, as a gift to her beloved sister, the original Queen of Atlantis.

The Atlantean Gemstones are not mere adornments; they possess a magical essence that transcends the boundaries of the ocean realm. Their extraordinary power lies in their ability to unlock the elusive gateway to the lost island of Atlantis. In the event that an ocean shifter finds themselves ensnared in the clutches of another realm, these enchanted rubies become their key to returning home.

To access this portal, one must hold both rubies and chant the incantation carved into the ancient Coral Tablets by the Sea Sorceress herself. The tablets were guarded in the hidden chambers of the Coral Palace, a place known only to the merfolk royals.

The lineage of the Atlantean Gemstones passed down through generations of merfolk royalty until fate led them into the possession of Princess Seraphina. A spirited mermaid, more inclined toward adventure than royal duties, Seraphina embarked on a journey to the human realm. Unfortunately, her adventurous spirit met a tragic end when she was ensnared in a human fishing net, and the precious rubies were believed lost for centuries.

It was not until Samantha Blue, a descendant of the sea, came into possession of the Atlantean Gemstones. Samantha's mother stumbled upon the rubies during an ocean swim, where they were washed into the rocks of a hidden pool. Recognizing the significance of these mystical gems, she bequeathed them to her only daughter, kindling a spark of hope to rediscover the long-lost island of Atlantis.

Samantha, uncertain of the state of Atlantis and its very existence, resisted the allure of the gemstones until circumstances left her no choice.

The Sea Diamond & The Sapphires

These enchanted jewels, forged in the heart of the underwater volcanoes, are intricately bound by a cosmic bond that ties them together for eternity. Carried together, the single diamond and double sapphires bear the weight of a profound purpose—to unlock a hidden portal concealed within a specific rock. This rock guards the coveted map leading to the island of Atlantis.

Samantha Blue unwittingly possessed this extraordinary trio of stones. Transformed into keyrings, the gems accompanied her through life, their true significance shrouded in the lost history of merfolk. Samantha remained unaware of the latent power they held and the destiny they harbored.

It wasn't until Cordelia and Wade embarked on the perilous quest to unveil the secrets of Atlantis, that the true purpose of the enchanted stones was revealed. Wade, attuned to the ancient whispers of the sea, recognized the stones and led them to an ancient pirate jail hidden along the coast.

In the heart of the jail, the jewels unlocked a concealed rock that, when moved aside, revealed the map to Atlantis. Yet, the map was not a mere parchment easily understood by mortal eyes. Its arcane symbols and hidden pathways could only be revealed through the touch of enchanted squid ink, and once the markings were revealed, could only be interpreted by a future oracle or member of the High Council.

The trio of stones, having fulfilled their destiny, now find their resting place in the great hall of Atlantis, alongside an array of other magical artifacts.

The White Pearl

Inside the walls of Atlantis, a mystical artifact known as the White Pearl emerged from the creative hands of the original High Council. This magical marvel was no ordinary gem; it was an enchanting orb, carefully embedded into an ornate mirror within the majestic great hall. Here, ocean shifters could call upon the council, seeking their wise advice and guidance, whenever they pleased.

However, the tranquility of this underwater utopia was shattered when the nefarious dragon kings overran the city, leading to the loss of both Atlantis and its cherished white pearl. For centuries, no one knew who had possession of the magical jewel.

The High Council, faced with the devastation wrought by the dragon kings, pronounced a solemn curse upon the ocean shifters. These aquatic beings were condemned to a life beneath the waves, separated from the splendors of the human world. The High Council, in response, withdrew to their timeless blue chamber, where they patiently waited for the day when the water species could be united once more and find their way to an audience.

The white pearl, imbued with a desire to be found, became a beacon of hope for the ocean shifters. The High Council, in turn, yearned for their subjects to prove themselves worthy of the artifact's magical gifts. In the realm of the human world, the white pearl unveils its powers only when two ocean shifters from opposing races join forces, utilizing its magic with pureness in their hearts.

Other Pearls

Pearls, formed from Cascadia's tears, embody profound magical energies. Functioning as mystical keys, these pearls safeguard the ocean's secrets and the essence of the ocean shifters. Among their sacred duties is the protection of the gateway to Atlantis. To unlock the Atlantean portal, the pearls must be unearthed in a specific sequence of colors: Black, followed by orange, and concluding with green.

Concealed within an ancient pirate jail along the Californian coast lies the elusive black pearl, entwined with the map of Atlantis. Upon seamlessly integrating the black pearl into a coral formation guarded by vigilant electric eels, the emergence of an orange pearl is unveiled. The journey continues to an underground ice cave near Mount Rainier, where the orange pearl unveils one of the Atlantean diamonds and reveals a companion green pearl. The final leg of the quest leads to the abyssal depths of the Mariana Trench, where the green pearl must be placed to unveil the second diamond.

Only by collecting and revealing these pearls in the prescribed order can the ocean shifters, as a united community, gather the two powerful diamonds and use them to retrace their ancestral paths to Atlantis.

The Atlantean Diamonds

The mystical diamonds serve as the gateway to the sacred portal leading to Atlantis. However, these precious treasures are not accessible to mere wanderers of the sea. The High Council understood that the ocean races, with their shifting forms, must refrain from returning to the island until a harmonious alliance among all aquatic beings was forged. Only then could the inherent magic within the diamonds be harnessed, requiring the presence of at least two distinct ocean shifter species.

To unlock the potent energy concealed within the gems, it is imperative that two individuals, epitomizing the pinnacle of their respective species, stand united in purpose. These chosen representatives must demonstrate unwavering unity, proving themselves as the paragons of their kind. Only through such a profound and genuine connection can the diamonds be activated, unveiling their formidable power and allowing passage to the legendary Atlantis.

The Golden Trident

The Trident of Atlantis is a legendary and powerful artifact steeped in mysticism and ancient Atlantean lore. The trident possesses incredible magical powers, making it one of the most sought-after relics in the city of Atlantis.

Forging the Trident

The Trident of Atlantis was forged in the heart of an underwater volcano, deep within the ocean's abyss by Vorago and his trusted blacksmith, Tidecaster. Tidecaster was known for his unparalleled mastery of metallurgy and enchantment, and he was chosen by Vorago to create a weapon that would symbolize the kingdom's strength and connection to the sea.

To forge the trident, Tidecaster ventured into the treacherous depths of the volcano, where molten lava flowed like rivers of fire. He used a combination of mystical metals found only in the heart of the ocean, such as Hydrastone and Aquagold, known for their unique properties that enhanced the trident's magical potential.

Tidecaster chanted ancient incantations as he hammered the metals together, calling upon Vorago to infuse the trident with his powers. The trident absorbed the essence of the sea, becoming a conduit for the very forces that ruled over Atlantis.

Magical Powers:

The Trident of Atlantis possesses a wide range of magical powers, each tied to the element of water and the sea:

Hydrokinesis:

The wielder of the trident gains the ability to manipulate water at will. They can create and control torrents, whirlpools, and tidal waves, making them a formidable force in battles both on land and underwater.

Aquatic Communication:

By touching the trident to the water's surface, the user can communicate with and command sea creatures, from the tiniest fish to the mightiest of sea serpents.

Water Breathing:

The trident bestows upon its wielder the ability to breathe underwater indefinitely, making them immune to the dangers of drowning.

Healing Waters:

When the trident is plunged into a body of water, it can cleanse and heal wounds and ailments, providing a source of rejuvenation and vitality.

Storm Manipulation:

In times of great need, the trident can call forth fierce storms and tempests, unleashing the wrath of the ocean's fury on adversaries.

Teleportation:

The trident can create watery portals, allowing the wielder to travel swiftly between different bodies of water, effectively covering vast distances instantaneously.

Tidal Control:

The wielder can raise or lower the tides, which can have a profound impact on coastal regions and naval battles.

Only those with a pure heart and a deep connection to the sea can harness the full extent of the trident's magical powers. The Trident of Atlantis remains a symbol of Atlantean heritage and their mastery over the aquatic realm, serving as both a protector of their city and a source of wonder for all who seek its secrets.

The Guardian Ring

This mystical ring, adorned with a radiant white pearl at its heart, is not just a piece of jewelry; it is the most cherished protector against the fearsome sea monsters that roam the ocean shifter realm.

The enchanted pearl is a relic passed down through generations of ocean shifters, whispered about in songs and revered in stories. This magical ring was crafted by the most skilled of their kind, in collaboration with wise seers who had visions of the perils that lurked in the depths. The pearl at its center is a symbol of purity, a beacon of hope that lights up the darkness of the ocean floor.

But what makes the enchanted pearl truly special is its remarkable power—a shimmering forcefield that it casts around those who possess it. This forcefield is a sanctuary, an impenetrable shield against the most dreaded of all sea creatures—The Hound of the Ocean.

The Hound of the Ocean is a colossal beast that dwells in the deepest trenches of the ocean, where the water pressure is crushing and the darkness is all-consuming. Its body is covered in impenetrable scales, and its eyes gleam with malevolence. It is a creature of nightmares, and it hungers for the taste of merfolk flesh.

When a merperson wears the enchanted pearl, its magic responds to the individual's thoughts and intentions. As the ominous silhouette of the hound approaches, the pearl glows with an ethereal light, casting a protective barrier around the merperson and their companions. The forcefield is a mesmerizing sight to behold, a shimmering, iridescent bubble that dances with the colors of the sea. Inside this enchanting sphere, ocean shifters are safe from the leviathan's reach.

To possess the enchanted pearl is a great honor and a heavy responsibility. Merfolk who are entrusted with its guardianship are chosen for their courage and wisdom. They dedicate their lives to safeguarding their community and maintaining the delicate balance of the underwater world. The ring last belonged to Cordelia Blue, Queen of Atlantis, but now resides with Gal Waters waiting for the fateful day when he will use it to propose.

Ice flute

The ice flute is a magical instrument delicately carved from the purest ice, hailing from the hands of one who possesses a profound connection with the orb of Ice and Snow. When its ethereal notes grace the air, they weave a hypnotic melody that not even the fiercest of seawolves can resist, succumbing to its enchanting spell as they are lulled into a deep, dreamless slumber. It is only then that the individual intended to wield Vorago's trident can sneak past the hypnotized guardians and use its power.

The Spear of the Merfolk

When merfolk first evolved they were free to roam the seas as well as land. However, most preferred the sanctuary of the ocean and using the ancient and reliable weapon of their species; the spear. Originally made from driftwood or mangrove trees readily available to the ocean shifters, the evolution of centuries saw the incorporation of diverse materials into the crafting of these spears. Coral, rock, granite, steel, and shells sanctified by the elusive eelusionists contributed to the arsenal of the gentle ocean dwellers.

Despite the relentless advancement of human weaponry that far surpassed the merfolk spear, these serene ocean shifters clung tenaciously to their ancestral weapon. They endeavored to enhance its capabilities, adapting and upgrading it over time. Upon the reclamation of Atlantis, the vigilant head of defense was determined to fortify the spear's prowess. Indestructible materials were sought, and ingenious incendiary devices were incorporated, imbuing the spears with newfound strength.

After being blessed by the Power of the Sea, these merfolk spears have become the most powerful weapons in ocean shifter history.

The Black Blinding Rock

In the clandestine gatherings of the malevolent Denizens of the Deep, dark rituals unfold, releasing arcane energies that ripple through the aquatic landscape. Under the most secret circumstances, these rituals give rise to remarkable stones, each imbued with an intention mirroring the sinister rites performed by the malevolent beings. Among these mystical creations, the blinding rock emerges as a gem of unparalleled significance, a crystalline embodiment of the nefarious magic that resides in the abyss.

Endowed with an eerie luminescence, the blinding rock harbors the power to unveil hidden realms of magic when introduced to the legendary Fountain of Youth nestled within the heart of Atlantis. The fusion of its ominous energies with the sacred waters transcends the boundaries of The Mermaid Chronicles, veiling both the revered prophecies and the wise oracle in an impenetrable shroud of enchantment, causing an inability to decipher the unfolding prophecies and unravel their true intent.

Despite its rarity, the blinding rock emerges as a potent artifact—a mystical tool that possesses the ability to shape destinies and alter the tides of fate. Its unparalleled power, however, comes with a chilling caveat, for in the grasp of those with malignant intentions, this gem becomes a harbinger of devastation, capable of distorting the fabric of the underwater world.

Among the merfolk, tales are whispered of daring quests undertaken by intrepid adventurers seeking the elusive blinding rock, drawn to its bewitching allure and the promise of unlocking the secrets hidden within the ocean's depths.

Squid Ink

For centuries, merfolk have harnessed the power of magical squid ink, a rare and potent substance found deep within the ocean, to unveil hidden truths on ancient maps.

This ink, harvested from enchanted squids dwelling in the abyssal depths, possesses a unique property. When applied to ancient maps, it reveals intricate details, long-lost pathways, and mysterious symbols.

The magical squid ink is delicately applied to the faded parchment. As the ink makes contact with the map, it comes to life, glowing with an ethereal luminescence. Trails of light illuminate forgotten paths, and symbols pulse with ancient power, guiding the merfolk on their quest. These maps, believed to be a gift from the sea deities, were the key to finding the lost island of Atlantis.

However, gathering squid ink is no easy feat. The last remnants were guarded by fierce electric eels, their bodies crackling with blue energy that can deter even the bravest of merfolk. These eels, enchanted by ancient sea magic, protect the secrets of the ink, ensuring that only those deemed worthy can approach and apply its use.

The last known vial of squid ink was uncovered by Cordelia Blue, Wade Waters, Trent Summers, Dylan Blue, Marina Waters, and Stephanie Bowers, and aided them in their path to finding Atlantis.

Coconut Magic

Merfolk have crafted a drink as enchanting as the underwater world itself. Coconut Magic is a concoction that embodies the essence of their mystical realm. This ethereal elixir, known only to ocean shifters, is a testament to their deep connection with the sea and the bounty it provides.

Coconut Magic is a shimmering potion made from the finest coconuts plucked from the palm trees that grace their coral gardens. With a delicate touch, they blend the sweet nectar of coconuts with the purest, crystal-clear waters of their ocean home,

infusing it with a hint of sea salt to capture the essence of the sea. To elevate its enchantment, they add a secret ingredient: the luminous pearls they gather from the ocean floor. These iridescent gems impart a subtle shimmer and a touch of the otherworldly to their creation. The result is a drink that glows like moonlight on the surface of the water, tasting of tropical dreams and the mysteries of the deep.

Coconut Magic is a symbol of their love for the ocean and its treasures, a testament to their enduring connection with the sea. Sipping this elixir is like sharing a piece of their underwater world, where merfolk dance among coral castles, and the tides sing a serenade to the heart of the ocean. It is a drink reserved for moments of celebration and reflection, a reminder that the magic of the sea flows through us, binding them to the depths in which they dwell.

Ghost pirates

The ghost pirates, previously a legion of ocean shifters, emerged from the shadows to pilfer the riches of Atlantis in the early days of its existence. Vorago, incensed by the betrayal after bestowing such a utopia upon these shifters, cast the mariners into a dimension far removed from their aquatic paradise. In a cruel twist, he cursed them to endure an eternal existence as undead entities, ceaselessly yearning for fulfillment that eternally eludes them.

Their ethereal vessel, a phantom ship woven from cobwebs and dust, sails through the void between dimensions. Through an unexpected twist of fate, they stumbled upon an unsettling revelation—the purity of children's innocence could bestow newfound strength upon their spectral vessel, enabling them to breach the veil and re-enter the realm of humankind. Thus, their unholy quest began: night after night, they would stealthily spirit away unsuspecting children, draining the very essence of their innocence, all in pursuit of a remedy to break free from their cursed state.

Seawolves

Seawolves are fierce underwater chimeras who guard the sacred trident of Vorago.

Long ago, when the oceans were wilder and the currents untamed, seawolves roamed freely through the depths after being saved from land and transformed into water animals. They were creatures of unparalleled beauty and terrifying might, with sleek, serpentine bodies that shimmered with colors unknown to the merfolk. Their eyes blazed like precious sapphires, and their teeth were as sharp as the coral that lined the abyssal trenches.

The seawolves were the chosen protectors of Vorago's trident. The mighty god of the ocean entrusted this divine artifact to the seawolves, believing in their unwavering loyalty.

For countless generations, the seawolves fulfilled their sacred duty with honor and pride. They kept the trident hidden deep within a labyrinthine rock fortress, shielded from all who sought to wield its might for selfish purposes. The merfolk revered them as the guardians of their realm, offering them treasures of the sea and songs of praise in return for their protection.

However, as the ages passed, the merfolk world began to change. Even before Atlantis was invaded by the dragon kings, and the merfolk and selachii were cursed to remain in the ocean, the seawolves crept quietly away to protect the power of the trident, fearing it would be used for selfish purposes by the ocean shifters. They believed the merfolk had forgotten the true purpose of the trident and had become too enamored with their own vanities.

It wasn't until Gal Waters, the guardian of the orb of Snow & Ice, sought out these fearsome beasts and mesmerized them with a flute carved from ice, that the seawolves relinquished their grasp on the ancient trident, recognizing Gal as the warrior he was becoming. They understood the purity in his heart, and after eons of playing sentry, were relieved to find a worthy wielder.

Denizens of the Deep

In the depths of the ocean, there exists a realm shrouded in enigma and terror. It is a realm ruled by the four dark and mysterious gods known as the Denizens of the Deep. To the merfolk, these ancient and powerful entities are both revered and feared, for they hold the keys to unimaginable power, capable of shaping the currents of existence beneath the waves.

The first of these godly beings is Dagonor, the Weaver of the Dark. Dagonor is said to have skin as dark as the abyss itself, with tendrils of inky blackness flowing from his form. He is the master of deception, a cunning trickster who can ensnare the minds of those who dare to challenge him. To be granted power by Dagonor is to be bestowed with the ability to manipulate the fabric of reality, to bend light and sound to one's will, and to become an unseen force in the watery depths.

The second god, Nautulan, the Whisperer of Tides, holds sway over the ebb and flow of the ocean's currents. Her presence is marked by the haunting melodies that drift through the underwater world, enchanting all who hears them. Those who seek her favor are blessed with the power to command the tides, to summon storms or still the raging seas, and to traverse vast distances with a mere thought.

Then there is Maelstroth, the Keeper of Currents. Maelstroth is an ancient and brooding deity, whose eyes are said to burn with an otherworldly fire. Those who dare to seek his wisdom are granted access to the hidden knowledge of the deep, the secrets of forgotten civilizations, and the power to tap into the essence of the ocean itself.

Last but not least is Karkenloth, the Lord of Leviathans. Karkenloth is a colossal being, a titan among gods, whose form is said to be a merging of all the creatures that dwell in the darkest reaches of the ocean. To be blessed by Karkenloth is to be granted dominion over the mightiest of sea beasts, to command their loyalty and wield their monstrous strength as one's own, and to become the most powerful version of oneself.

The ocean shifters whisper tales of these four gods in hushed tones, for they know that to seek their favor is to court danger and temptation in equal measure. The Denizens of the Deep are ancient and fickle, their motives inscrutable, and their power beyond reckoning. Yet, for those brave enough to tread the path of darkness, the allure of such boundless power is too great to resist.

Sea witches

These beings are born from the dark and turbulent emotions of jealousy and envy. These tales serve as cautionary stories for the merfolk, reminding them of the dangers that lurk beneath the waves.

The transformation of a mermaid into a sea witch begins with the seed of jealousy and envy taking root in their heart. It often starts innocently enough—perhaps a mermaid covets the beauty, talents, or possessions of another. As these negative emotions fester and grow, they manifest themselves physically in the mermaid's appearance and abilities.

Transformation:

The transformation from a graceful mermaid into a sea witch is a gradual and eerie process. Scales that were once vibrant and iridescent begin to darken and lose their luster. The mermaid's once-glistening tail becomes gnarled and twisted, taking on the

appearance of serpentine scales. This transformation is symbolic of the corruption that jealousy and envy can bring to one's soul.

Snakes for Hair:

One of the most terrifying aspects of a sea witch's appearance is her hair. Instead of the flowing locks of a mermaid, a sea witch's hair turns into a writhing mass of serpents. These snakes are a reflection of the mermaid's envy, constantly whispering poisonous thoughts and planting seeds of discord.

Terrifying Abilities:

As jealousy and envy consume the mermaid, they gain access to dark and terrifying abilities. Sea witches are known to control the turbulent currents of the ocean, conjure storms, evoke sea monsters, and manipulate marine life to do their bidding. They use these powers to exact revenge on those they are envious of or to sow chaos and discord among the merfolk community.

Isolation and Ostracization:

Once a mermaid fully transforms into a sea witch, she becomes an outcast among her kind. The merfolk fear her dark powers and the malevolent influence she exudes. Sea witches often live in underwater caves thick kelp forests, far from the vibrant and harmonious merfolk communities.

Seeking Redemption:

Some merfolk legends hold that there is a way for a sea witch to redeem herself and return to her mermaid form. This typically involves acts of selflessness, repentance, and seeking forgiveness from those she has wronged. However, the path to redemption is treacherous and rarely achieved.

In the world of merfolk, the creation of a sea witch serves as a stark warning about the destructive power of jealousy and envy. Mermaids are encouraged to nurture positive emotions and avoid the dark path that leads to becoming a sea witch.

Lady of the lake

The Lady of the Lake is a mythical figure who has fascinated the world above the waves for centuries.

The Birth of the Lady

According to merfolk lore, the Lady of the Lake was not always a lady. She was born from the very heart of the ocean itself, a creation of the tides and the moon's gentle caress. As the daughter of Vorago, the mighty sea god, and Selene, the moon goddess, she embodied the mystical union of earth and water, night and day.

Her Enchanted Lake

The Lady of the Lake, known to us as Eudora, found her home in a hidden, underwater cavern, a place of ethereal beauty where the boundaries between worlds blurred. Her enchanted lake, Lacuna Aeternum (The Eternal Gap), was a realm where time flowed differently, and the waters held the power to grant wisdom and bestow mighty gifts to those who dared to seek her out.

The Sword Excalibur

One of the most famous tales surrounding the Lady of the Lake is the bestowal of King Arthur's legendary sword, Excalibur. In the merfolk version of the story, Eudora gifted the sword to Arthur not as a mere weapon but as a symbol of the harmony between land and sea. Excalibur's blade was said to be forged from the heart of a fallen star, and its power was unmatched, a reflection of the Lady's divine grace.

Merfolk Protectors

As the guardian of Lacuna Aeternum, Eudora held the ocean's deepest secrets and was revered by merfolk as their protector. In times of great peril, they believed her spirit would rise from the depths, riding upon the crests of mighty waves, to shield them from harm and to calm the tempestuous seas.

The Lady's Disappearance

Tragedy struck when, in a time of great upheaval, the entrance to Lacuna Aeternum was sealed off, cutting off the Lady of the Lake from the world above. Hearts wept for the guardian, but the merfolk understood she had retreated to protect the sanctity of her realm from the chaos that threatened to consume it. It is known that she now resides in the secluded lakes of the Lake District in England. She will not leave her new home, but an ocean shifter in need may visit her there and seek her ancient wisdom.

Ashrays

Resembling mutated stingrays, the Ashrays are ethereal beings, their bodies a mesmerizing fusion of translucence and ghostly white hues. But do not be deceived by their delicate appearance, for they are the embodiment of terror, haunting the depths only under the cover of night.

When the sun sets and the ocean's surface darkens, ocean shifters sense the impending danger. They know the ashrays will soon glide silently through the shadows, seeking their prey with unmatched precision. The shifters feel their hearts quicken as they hear the distant whisper of the ashrays' approach, a sound akin to the rustle of ghostly silk against the water.

The mere touch of these spectral hunters inflicts burns that sear like fire and infections that linger for an agonizing year, a reminder of their lethal presence. The favorite prey of ashrays is the selachii, directed by the High Council to inflict punishment on them for losing the beloved island of Atlantis. Ashrays cannot be killed, only tolerated, and no repelling agent has yet been discovered.

Whirlpool prisons

The High Council of Atlantis, comprised of the most influential and skilled leaders of the underwater city, was known for maintaining order and justice. Before the time of the dragon king mutiny, when the council deemed it necessary to imprison those who posed a threat to the harmony of Atlantis, they turned to the ancient and formidable dragon shifters for assistance. The dragon kings, known for their mastery over water and their deep understanding of its forces, possessed the knowledge and ability to create powerful whirlpool prisons.

Here's how the process unfolds:

Council's Decision:

The High Council of Atlantis convenes a solemn assembly to discuss the fate of a dangerous individual or group that threatens the serenity of their underwater kingdom. It could be a rogue merperson, a group of sea creatures, or any entity that poses a significant threat.

Council's Request:

The council must unanimously agree that the intended subject is guilty of accused crimes and deserves to be imprisoned for a set amount of time.

Gathering the Elements:

The dragon king member of the High Council (or another if the member is unavailable) begins to gather the necessary elements and materials from the depths of the ocean. They collect enchanted corals, crystals, and exotic sea flora known only to them. These materials serve as the foundation for the whirlpool prison's magic.

Ritualistic Magic:

Under the light of the bioluminescent creatures that inhabit the darkest depths, the dragon king performs an intricate and powerful ritual. They invoke the ancient sea gods and channel the energy of the ocean itself to create a swirling vortex of water, which will serve as the prison.

Containment of Threat:

As the whirlpool prison takes shape, the High Council provides information about the target to be imprisoned. The dragon king uses their mastery over water to infuse the vortex with protective spells and wards, ensuring that only those intended for imprisonment are drawn into its depths.

Activation:

With a final incantation, the dragon king activates the whirlpool prison. It comes to life with an otherworldly luminescence, its waters swirling with incredible force. It becomes invisible to all but those who possess the knowledge of its existence.

Secure Imprisonment:

The intended target, now trapped within the whirlpool prison, finds themselves in a watery abyss, unable to escape the relentless currents. The prison is designed to prevent any escape attempts, and only the High Council and the dragon king who created it have the means to release someone from its grasp.

These whirlpool prisons are both a symbol of the merfolk's commitment to justice and a testament to the mysterious and powerful forces that govern their world. They serve as a reminder that even in the depths of the ocean, order and harmony must be maintained to protect the delicate balance of their underwater realm.

It should be noted that in recent times none of the ritualistic ingredients have been necessary to create the whirlpool, such was the power of evolution among the small, but mighty number of dragon kings.

Telepathy

In the world of ocean shapeshifters, telepathy operates as a unique and vital form of communication, allowing merfolk and selachii to connect on a deep, intuitive level regardless of their physical forms. This telepathic ability is intricately linked to their aquatic environment and their shapeshifting abilities.

Connection through Water

Ocean shapeshifters possess a heightened sensitivity to the properties of water, which plays a crucial role in their telepathic abilities. Water is seen as a conductor and amplifier of their thoughts and emotions. When they are submerged in water, their telepathic potential is greatly enhanced.

Shapeshifting Catalyst

Shapeshifting itself is the catalyst for their telepathy. When a merfolk or selachii transitions between their aquatic and human-like forms, it triggers a surge in their psychic energy. This energy connects them to others of their kind who are also in proximity to water, opening a telepathic channel.

Mental Resonance

The telepathic connection is based on mental resonance. Ocean shapeshifters must establish a mental link with one another, and this is often initiated by focusing their thoughts and emotions on a specific individual. It's as though they are tuning their psychic "frequency" to match that of the intended recipient.

Emotion-Based Communication

Emotions play a significant role in their telepathy. While they can transmit thoughts and concepts, emotions are conveyed more powerfully. This emotional depth allows for a profound understanding of each others' feelings, fostering empathy and unity among their kind.

Range and Limitations

The range of telepathic communication is limited to a certain distance from the source of water. The farther they are from a significant body of water, the weaker the connection becomes. Additionally, the telepathy is most effective among members of the same shapeshifter species but can be extended to other aquatic creatures to a limited extent.

Shared Experiences

As ocean shapeshifters traditionally lived their lives beneath the waves, they often shared their experiences, knowledge, and stories through telepathy. This allows for the rapid spread of information and helps them adapt to changes in their underwater environment.

Private vs· Group Communication

Ocean shapeshifters can engage in both private and group telepathic conversations. Private communication involves a one-on-one connection, while group communication involves several individuals forming a collective mental link to share thoughts, emotions, and ideas simultaneously.

Telepathy is not just a means of communication; it's an essential part of their culture and survival. It allows them to maintain a deep sense of community, share their rich underwater world, and adapt to the ever-changing challenges of the ocean environment.

Echomancer's Embrace
(The Resuscitation Ritual)

Among the most treasured abilities of merfolk and selachii is the power to bestow the gift of shifting upon a drowning human in need of salvation.

The Echomancer's Embrace is a sacred rite passed down through generations, guarded closely by the ocean shapeshifters.

The Call of the Abyss

When a human is in dire peril, their cries for help echo through the ocean's currents, resonating with the ocean shapeshifters' empathic abilities. They can sense the distress and are drawn to the location where their help is needed.

The Confluence

As an ocean shapeshifter arrives at the scene, they embrace the struggling human, their beautiful tails casting an ethereal glow in the depths. They harmonize with the natural rhythms of the ocean, tapping into its energy.

The Shifter's Heartbeat

The ocean shifter begins a telepathic chant, their voice blending with the soothing sounds of the sea. This chant represents the heartbeat of the ocean, the life force that binds all aquatic creatures.

The Bubble of Transformation

The Echomancer then commands the ocean's currents to gather around the drowning human, forming a delicate, shimmering bubble. This bubble is the heart of the ritual, the vessel of transformation. Inside, it contains a mixture of seawater, air, and the Echomancer's own essence, creating a magical elixir. Smaller bubbles surround the pair and offer safety while the transformation takes place.

The Shifter's Breath

With a graceful gesture, the Echomancer sends a stream of air into the bubble. This breath of life mixes with the elixir, and the water within the bubble starts to shimmer and pulse with an otherworldly energy.

The Exchange of Essence

As the bubble gently envelops the drowning human, their body begins to undergo a profound transformation. Their legs fuse together into a strong, iridescent tail, covered in scales that match the color of their newfound shifting clan. Gills form on their ribs, allowing them to breathe underwater.

The Awakening

The newly transformed shifter opens his or her eyes within the bubble, their connection to the ocean deepening with every passing moment. They can sense the currents and communicate telepathically with other ocean shifters.

The Bond

They become part of a larger community, and their purpose is to protect the oceans, just as the ocean shapeshifters have done for centuries, and are tasked with saving other humans who find themselves in equally dire situations.

The Ascension

Finally, the bubble bursts, releasing the fully transformed ocean shifter into his or her new life beneath the waves. They are welcomed into the clan, and the ocean shapeshifters continue to teach them the secrets of their newfound abilities, ensuring they become a guardian of the deep.

Reproduction

Merfolk and other ocean shifters are not like ordinary beings; their lives are bound to the ebb and flow of the sea, and their reproduction is a unique and enchanting process. Unlike the common perception that merfolk emerged from clam shells, their origins are far more intricate.

Within their realm, merfolk are divided into two distinct genders: males and females. Each merperson possesses the ability to shift between their aquatic and humanoid forms at will, a gift bestowed upon them by the ancient sea deities. While the merfolk appear ageless and eternal, they do indeed age, but at a much slower pace than humans.

Reproduction among shifters while in their aquatic form is a deeply romantic and ritualistic affair. It begins with the call of the ocean itself, as the currents sing a melodious tune that resonates through the underwater world. This mesmerizing song serves as a beacon to summon the merfolk together. As the male and female merfolk gather, they swim in graceful circles, their tails intertwining as they dance to the rhythm of the sea.

Amidst the undulating seaweed and colorful corals, the merfolk engage in a courtship that is nothing short of magical. Their eyes meet, and a connection forms that transcends the boundaries of time and space. It is as though their souls have been intertwined since the dawn of creation.

In the heart of their courtship, the male presents the female with a precious gift—a pearl of unparalleled beauty and rarity. This pearl is a symbol of their love and devotion, a token of their promise to create life together in the embrace of the ocean.

Once their bond is sealed, the merfolk couple venture to the ancient coral gardens, where they carefully select a suitable nest for their offspring. Within the depths of the coral nest, the female lays a cluster of translucent, opalescent eggs. These eggs are the

embodiment of their love and are infused with the magic of the sea.

The male stands guard, using his powerful tail to create a protective barrier around the eggs. For weeks, they watch over their precious progeny, sharing stories and songs, and whispering sweet words of affection to one another.

As time passes, the eggs begin to glow with a serene light, and a gentle hum fills the water around them. This is the sign that their offspring are ready to hatch. With great anticipation, the merfolk couple witness the emergence of tiny, fragile mermaid fry, each no larger than a seashell. The newborns possess a combination of their parents' traits, with scales that shimmer like the sea and eyes that sparkle like starlight.

The merfolk parents nurture their young, teaching them the ways of the ocean, the ancient songs, and the secrets of the deep. As the merfolk fry grow and thrive, the cycle of life continues, and the ocean's magic remains intact, ensuring the survival of their race.

In this enchanting world beneath the waves, merfolk reproduction is a testament to the enduring power of love, the mystical connection between two souls, and the profound beauty of the ocean's secrets.

Note: cross species reproduction is only possible when the male and female are in their human forms.

Second Note: when in human forms, reproduction follows the human pattern.

Funerals

When it comes to honoring an ocean shapeshifter who has transitioned from the physical realm, the merfolk community comes together to celebrate their life and bid them farewell in a unique and symbolic way.

The Preparation

Upon the passing of an ocean shapeshifter, the community gathers near the shoreline, where the body of the departed shapeshifter is carefully prepared for the ceremony, adorned with beautiful seaweed garlands and precious pearls, signifying the individual's connection to the ocean's treasures.

The Pyre

A pyre, made of driftwood and adorned with bioluminescent sea plants, is constructed on a sturdy raft, floating gently on the surface of the water. The pyre represents the transformative nature of life, with the drifting wood symbolizing the eternal cycle of the ocean and all its inhabitants. The body of the departed ocean

shapeshifter is placed upon the pyre, positioned with care and respect.

The Ceremony

As the sun sets, casting a warm, golden glow upon the ocean's surface, the merfolk community gathers around the pyre. The High Council and senate lead the ceremony, chanting ancient hymns that echo through the water, creating a melodic harmony that resonates with the essence of the ocean. The songs tell tales of the shapeshifter's adventures, their kindness, and their connection to the vast, mysterious depths.

Pushing the Pyre into the Ocean

With great reverence, the people come forward, their tails swaying gracefully in the currents. They gently push the pyre into the ocean, allowing it to float away, symbolizing the shapeshifter's journey into the afterlife. The raft, adorned with flowers and candles, bobs on the surface, carried by the gentle waves.

Lighting the Pyre

As the pyre begins to drift away, a skilled merfolk with the power of fire, or a dragon king, conjures a flickering flame using their mystical abilities. The flame dances and leaps, gracefully touching the pyre. The wood catches fire, creating a mesmerizing display of light and warmth against the darkening waters.

Final Farewell

The community watches as the pyre, now ablaze with vibrant flames, becomes a beacon of light on the surface of the ocean. The ocean shifters sing a final, heartfelt song, their voices harmonizing with the crackling of the fire and the whispers of the sea.

In this solemn and beautiful ceremony, the shifters bid farewell to their fellow ocean friend, acknowledging their eternal connection to the ocean and celebrating the profound impact they had on their community. As the flames gradually fade and the pyre becomes a smoldering ember, the people disperse, carrying the memory of their beloved shapeshifter friend in their hearts.

Atlantis' Lament

In the depths of the deep blue sea,
Where the coral blooms and the waves run free,
Lived our queen, Cordelia, so fair,
A mermaid's grace, beyond compare.

With her flowing tail and her silver hair,
She ruled Atlantis, just and fair,
Her heart was pure, her spirit strong,
In her presence, we all belonged.

Oh, Cordelia, our mermaid queen,
In your memory, we still dream,
Of the days when you ruled the sea,
Now you're gone, and we're lost at sea.

But beneath the waves, a darkness grew,
A traitor lurked, a selachii so untrue,
He plotted schemes, with envy's flame,
To steal our queen's eternal name.

Cordelia, she trusted all,
Even as the shadows began to fall,
But betrayal struck, a deadly blow,
Took her life, let our tears flow.

Oh, Cordelia, our mermaid queen,
In your memory, we still dream,
Of the days when you ruled the sea,
Now you're gone, and we're lost at sea.

The ocean's depths, they echo your name,
In every heart, your love remains,
Atlanteans weep for what's been done,
A broken kingdom, forever undone.

Now the kingdom mourns, a somber song,
As we swim in the currents, trying to belong,
To the memory of a queen so dear,
Whose absence we'll forever fear.

In the waves, her spirit lives on,
In the moonlit tides, and the early dawn,
We'll honor her, our love so true,
For Cordelia, our hearts renew.

Oh, Cordelia, our mermaid queen,
In your memory, we still dream,
Of the days when you ruled the sea,
Now you're gone, and we're lost at sea.

In the depths of Atlantis, our tears we cry,
For our beloved queen, beneath the sky,
Though she's gone, her legacy remains,
In our hearts, in the sea's gentle chains.

PART THREE

SIGNIFICANT FIGURES

Vorago

Born from the ancient magic of the sea itself, the ocean's shapeshifters possessed an extraordinary ability to transform their fluid bodies into an array of aquatic forms. But what set them apart from all other creatures beneath the waves was their unwavering belief in a deity they had never seen, yet revered above all others—the mighty Vorago.

For countless generations, the ocean shapeshifters wove together a rich tapestry of myths and legends about their enigmatic god. Vorago is the creator of their world, the sculptor of the ocean's depths, and the master of tempestuous tides. Although Vorago has never shown himself to these devoted beings, his presence is felt in every current, every wave, and every whisper of the ocean's secrets.

Vorago descended from the heavens eons ago, and created a trident that shimmered like the moonlight on the water's surface. With a single, mighty thrust, he plunged the trident into the heart of the sea, giving life to the waters and all the creatures that inhabited them. His divine touch transformed shapeless matter into the vibrant coral reefs, the elusive sea creatures, and even the ocean shapeshifters themselves. The ocean's ever-changing beauty is a reflection of Vorago's boundless creativity and power.

The ocean shapeshifters worship Vorago through songs, dances, and rituals passed down through the ages. These offerings of devotion will keep their underwater paradise thriving and protect them from the wrath of Vorago's legendary anger. For when Vorago is pleased, he sends gentle currents and bountiful schools of fish, ensuring the ocean shapeshifters never go hungry. But when he is angered, the seas rage, and terrible storms would whip through the underwater realms, reminding the ocean shapeshifters of their god's mighty fury.

Their belief in Vorago's unseen presence runs deep, and they consider themselves the chosen guardians of his aquatic domain. It is their sacred duty to maintain the delicate balance of the sea, nurturing its life and preserving its mysteries. In return, they hope that one day, Vorago will reveal himself to them in all his divine glory.

Cascadia

Cascadia is a female goddess of water, the sister of Vorago, and the embodiment of the ocean's essence. While Vorago controlled the raging storms, the tumultuous waves, and the depths of the abyss, his sister's dominion lays in the heart and soul of the waters themselves.

She is a guardian of balance and harmony in the seas. Her touch can turn the most violent tempest into a gentle breeze, and she can calm the fiercest maelstroms with a mere glance. It is she who watches over the delicate ecosystems beneath the waves, nurturing the vibrant coral reefs, guiding the graceful dance of the jellyfish, and ensuring the survival of the tiniest plankton that forms the foundation of ocean life.

But the most captivating aspect of this goddess is her ability to shapeshift seamlessly between the forms of sea creatures. She is the ultimate chameleon of the deep, able to slip into the skin of a playful dolphin to frolic in the waves or don the guise of a sleek swordfish to dart through the ocean currents at incredible speeds. This gift allows her to intimately understand the lives and struggles of her subjects, the ocean shapeshifters.

She is said to dwell in a hidden palace made of luminescent

coral deep within uncharted waters, where the pressure was crushing, and the darkness absolute. There, she communes with her brother Vorago through the language of the sea, their voices carried by the currents across vast distances, invisible to all but the most attuned ocean shapeshifters.

The goddess watches over the ocean shifters, guiding their movements and ensuring the delicate balance of their world. When great challenges or threats arise in the ocean, they invoke her name in their songs and dances, asking for her wisdom and protection.

Despite their unwavering faith, the ocean shapeshifters had never seen the goddess, for she remains a mysterious and elusive figure, hidden in the depths of the ocean, her presence felt only through the undeniable beauty and power of the sea itself.

Tempest

Tempest is Vorago's brother.

The history of Tempest stretches back eons, long before the first merfolk graced the underwater realms. It is said that when the primordial waters were first formed, Tempest emerged from the tumultuous waves, a manifestation of the relentless and untamable force of water.

Tempest's powers are as vast and immeasurable as the endless ocean. He holds dominion over the storms both over the ocean and on land and can bridge the gap between the two. It is he who suggested to Vorago that ocean shifters should have the ability to leave the ocean and explore the continents. He is also responsible for developing the communication method of telepathy so that ocean shifters can commune beneath the waves.

Despite his fierce appearance and his control over the most extreme weather, Tempest is a gentle soul. He often meddles in shifter affairs, encouraging lightness and laughter in his people, although he has never revealed himself and no one has ever set eyes on him.

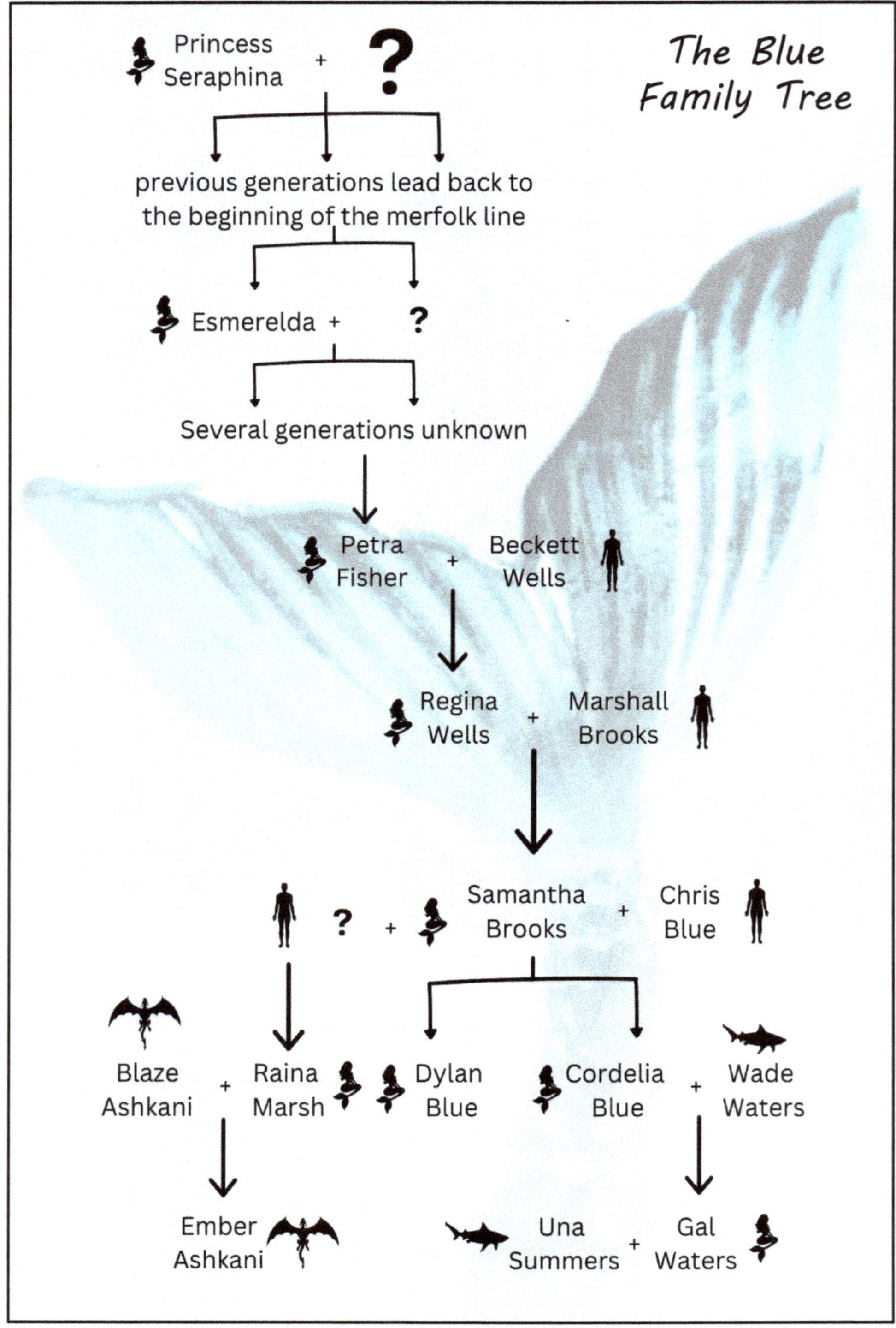

Princess Seraphina
+
?
The Blue Family Tree
previous generations lead back to the beginning of the merfolk line
Esmerelda + ?
Several generations unknown
Petra Fisher
+
Beckett Wells
Regina Wells
+
Marshall Brooks
?
+
Samantha Brooks
+
Chris Blue
Blaze Ashkani
+
Raina Marsh
Dylan Blue
Cordelia Blue
+
Wade Waters
Ember Ashkani
Una Summers
+
Gal Waters

Samantha Blue (nee Brooks)

Samantha Blue hails from the most ancient lineage of merfolk, standing as the designated heir to the regal dynasty. Orphaned at a tender age, she emerged as the sole surviving mermaid capable of treading on land, a unique ability she shared only with her three offspring. The firstborn, a consequence of a violent encounter, found refuge in an alternative abode. This decision, not born out of an inability to love a child forged in strife but rather driven by the ominous foretellings within The Mermaid Chronicles, aimed to shield the newborn from the perilous realm of shifter conflicts by placing them in a landlocked sanctuary.

Following the birth of the twins, Cordelia and Dylan, Samantha ruefully reconsidered her initial choice to part with her eldest progeny and embarked on a quest to reunite with them. However, her pursuit faced an abrupt interruption when Zale assaulted her during a boat voyage with her family. Concealing her merfolk heritage from her children, Samantha, aware that only the Fountain of Youth could mend her grievous injuries, utilized her personal keys to travel to Atlantis. Time constraints denied her the opportunity for farewells or the disclosure of vital secrets.

Upon reaching Atlantis and imbibing the last drops of the rejuvenating fountain, she discovered the island in ruins, a consequence of centuries of dragon kings' misrule. Ensnared as a captive for six arduous years, Samantha's liberation arrived when

Cordelia and Wade located her. A jubilant reunion unfolded with the twins and her spouse. Subsequently, her eldest daughter, Raina, arrived in Atlantis, and was welcomed into the fold with open arms. Samantha, now a wise member of the senate, opts to remain in Atlantis, never straying too far from her cherished family.

Dr Christopher Blue

Dr. Christopher Blue, a brilliant marine biologist, embarked on a journey of discovery that would forever alter the course of his life. Unbeknownst to him, his beloved wife, Samantha, concealed a captivating secret—a lineage of merfolk.

Tragedy struck with the force of a tempest when Chris lost his wife and their son in a harrowing shark attack. Grief threatened to consume him, but he found his anchor in the form of his young daughter, Cordelia. The weight of responsibility fell upon his shoulders as he realized he could not afford to lose himself, for Cordelia still needed him. The loss of Samantha Blue was a chasm in his heart that could never be filled, but he resolved to help Cordelia face her fears and combat the anxiety that plagued her.

As a dedicated father, Chris channeled his energies into understanding the source of Cordelia's anxiety. He turned his attention to sharks and a hormone they released, exploring the potential of adapting it into medication to alleviate the suffering of humans grappling with anxiety disorders. It was his way of honoring Samantha's memory and supporting Cordelia through her ordeal, or so he thought.

Little did Chris know that his daughter had unraveled the enigma of her mermaid ancestry and had discovered her long-lost brother, Dylan, was still alive.

Worries gnawed at his heart, fearing that Cordelia's newfound connection with Wade might not be as wholesome as he hoped. The revelation of the ocean shifters, their reunion with their legs, and the trials they had endured only added to his concerns.

With a heavy but supportive heart, Chris eventually granted his blessing for Cordelia and Wade to embark on a quest to find Atlantis. However, he insisted that they wait until they completed their high-school education. Chris played an instrumental role in assisting Nerida's escape from his Navy laboratory and concealing any traces that Cordelia and Wade left behind.

While unable to accompany them to the Puget Sound for the recovery of the first key to Atlantis, Chris felt immense relief when Gal, a dragon king High Council member, stepped in to mentor Cordelia and safeguard her from the clutches of vicious ice demons. The second leg of their perilous journey involved using a submersible accessible only to Chris, which took them to the murky depths of the Mariana Trench. Tragedy loomed yet again when the submersible malfunctioned, and Chris found himself on the precipice of drowning. In a remarkable turn of events, Wade performed a resuscitation ritual that not only saved Chris but transformed him into a selachii.

As a newly transformed selachii, Chris found solace in Mermaid Lagoon, where he dwelled alongside Maya and other merfolk. His love for the ocean deepened, and he became entrenched in the enchanting world of merfolk. When the time came to open the portal to Atlantis, Chris stood shoulder to shoulder with his daughter in the battle against the dragon kings, a testament to the unyielding love that bound their family.

Once the tumultuous battle was won, Chris was joyously reunited with Samantha, who had been a captive on the lost island. The family unit was restored, and they faced a promising future together. Chris stood by his daughter as she ruled over the island and was proud of Samantha when she took her place in the senate.

Reinvigorated by his experiences and newfound understanding of the ocean's secrets, Chris rekindled his passion for marine biology. He devoted his time to documenting the astonishing sea life around the island, becoming a mentor to Wade's sister, Marina, as she embarked on her own journey of discovery. His days are spent immersed in the world of the ocean's gentle creatures, yet he remains ever vigilant, ready to join the battle when the need arises.

Though his heart still aches from the loss of his daughter, Chris finds solace in the enduring presence of his son and the joy of bonding with his grandson. His life has transformed from an ordinary marine biologist to an integral part of the world of ocean shifters, where the secrets of the ocean are his to explore, and the love of his family is his most cherished treasure.

Cordelia Blue

Born into the ancient lineage of mermaid royalty, Cordelia's journey began in a tempest of tragedy. Unlike her peers, she didn't discover her mermaid tail during puberty but lived as a land-dweller, blissfully ignorant of her aquatic heritage. Fate's cruel hand was revealed when her twin brother and mother seemingly met their demise in a brutal attack. Traumatized, Cordelia shunned the water, despite her promising swimming career, until the impending arrival of her eighteenth birthday compelled her to confront her phobia. It was during her courageous confrontation with her fears, that she unearthed her identity as a mermaid.

Her awakening led to a revelation both miraculous and heart-wrenching: her twin brother, alive but trapped in the ocean, unable to shift onto land. Transformed through a resuscitation ritual after a vicious assault by Zale, he shared with Cordelia a sacred trust—a white pearl, a mystical key to seek counsel with the High Council. Their mission: to implore the return of their lost shapeshifting abilities. Along this perilous path, Cordelia found love in Wade, a selachii whose identity was as extraordinary as hers.

Their love story unfolded amidst challenges, betrayal, and interference, testing the bounds of their relationship, but they triumphed over all and returned the ability to shift to human form to all merfolk and selachii.

The quest for Atlantis emerged as Cordelia's next odyssey, demanding the discovery of magical keys to unlock a long-hidden portal. In the face of adversity, including the menacing presence of Stephanie, Wade's former flame, Cordelia's courage shone. She braved elemental threats, including an encounter with an ice demon, in which she almost met her end. It was her mentor, Gal, and the Power of the Sea that saved her and granted her command over fire.

Defeating the formidable dragon kings guarding Atlantis with her new fiery power, Cordelia restored the island to its former glory, reuniting with her captive mother. The reunion was bittersweet, for the ocean harbored more challenges. A devastating nuclear war laid waste to the mainland, leaving Cordelia, now pregnant with

Gal, to navigate a world in turmoil. She sought allies, including her former high-school nemesis, Babette, in a battle against sea witches and the Hound of the Ocean.

Cordelia's indomitable spirit persevered through battles and heartbreaks. A confrontation with the vengeful sea witch Stephanie and her ally, Aquaria, threatened all ocean shifters. The beach battleground became a crucible, testing Cordelia's resolve. In the end, love triumphed over jealousy and hatred. Cordelia and Wade embraced the survivors, welcoming humans into the sanctuary of Atlantis.

However, peace was short-lived. The ghost pirates emerged, stealing children from Atlantis, including Cordelia's young son, Gal. Cordelia embarked on a desperate quest, fueled by maternal determination and supported by her unwavering love for Wade. Their journey was fraught with peril, yet their bond remained unbreakable.

The battle against the ghost pirates was monumental, revealing treachery orchestrated by Zale, a dark force intertwined with Cordelia's destiny. Blinded by the misguided actions of an orcana member, Cordelia faced the ghost pirates and Zale, ultimately sacrificing herself for the safety of her son.

Cordelia's legacy endures, immortalized in the annals of ocean shapeshifter history. Her bravery, love, and sacrifice became a beacon of hope for generations to come, reminding all that even in the face of darkness, the power of love and courage can illuminate the deepest abyss and inspire others to follow in her courageous wake.

Dylan Blue

Dylan was born under the silvery glow of the moon, a twin to Cordelia, destined for extraordinary adventures. Before the age of thirteen, he was confronted by the malevolent selachii, Zale, whose nefarious motives aimed to snuff out the essence of Dylan's existence. In a desperate bid to extinguish his bloodline and seize control of the keys to Atlantis, Zale unleashed a brutal attack upon young Dylan. As death loomed, a courageous mermaid named Nerida intervened, performing a daring resuscitation ritual that saved his life but forever transformed him into a merman, and

only months before the natural transition would have occurred that would have allowed him to walk on land.

Embracing his newfound merman identity, Dylan found solace in the embrace of the Mermaid Lagoon, an enchanting underwater cavern that served as the sanctuary for merfolk along the west

coast of America. Here, he learned the ancient ways of his people, yearning for the day when his sister Cordelia would join him in the majestic depths of the ocean.

After five long years, Dylan's wish was granted, and he was reunited with his sister. Together, they embarked on a perilous quest to safeguard the magical white pearl, a precious artifact that held immense power. With the pearl in Cordelia's possession, Dylan stood by her side, guarding it against the selachii who hungered for its secrets. Their journey led them to uncover the pearl's mysteries, a discovery they hoped would pave the way for merfolk to regain their shifter legs and reconnect with their lost pasts.

Dylan's bravery and wisdom played a pivotal role in navigating the delicate alliances between merfolk and selachii. Despite his initial reservations about Cordelia's relationship with the selachii prince, Wade Waters, Dylan recognized the importance of unity in the face of adversity. His guidance proved invaluable, leading to a harmonious alliance that transcended the boundaries of their respective worlds.

When the curse binding their legs was finally broken, Dylan, along with his fellow merfolk and selachii, found themselves on the

unfamiliar shores of the human world. Struggling to adapt after his prolonged absence, he sought comfort in the arms of Babette, a human whose presence offered him fleeting solace amid the challenges of the surface world. But more often than not, Dylan found himself at the bottom of a bottle.

He played a vital role in recovering the magical pearls that unlocked the portal to Atlantis, facing off against formidable foes such as the dragon kings who guarded the ancient land. In a moment of selflessness, he performed the same resuscitation ritual that had saved him on Maya, transforming her into a mermaid and granting her a new lease on life. After the battle, Dylan and his sister Cordelia were reunited with their mother, whom they thought had been killed by Zale.

Yet, the passage of time did little to heal the wounds within Dylan's soul. The scars of loss and the haunting memories of battles left him tormented, seeking solace in the depths of alcohol and the tumultuous embrace of his relationship with Babette. Despite their deep connection, their love story was marred by the shadows of Dylan's past, casting a pall over their happiness.

When the horrors of nuclear war erupted on the mainland, Dylan once again found himself at the forefront of a mission to maintain peace in Atlantis. His bravery resurfaced as he faced the challenges head-on, rekindling his relationship with Babette amid the chaos. Together, they fought against the Hound of the Ocean and the malevolent sea witches, Aquaria and Stephanie.

In the ensuing years of peace, Dylan's inner tempest raged on, a storm of anguish and despair that no tranquility could quell. His struggle with PTSD and the weight of his past burdens left him drowning in the depths of depression. Despite Babette's unwavering support, their relationship reached an impasse, forcing her to leave Atlantis in pursuit of her own dreams.

The turning point in Dylan's life came with the arrival of his nephew, a beacon of innocence and hope in the merman's rocky existence. When the young boy was captured by malevolent ghost pirates, Dylan's fierce protectiveness emerged, compelling him to become the guardian of the elemental orb of Air & Flight.

Reluctantly embracing his newfound powers, he helped lead the charge against the sinister pirates, ultimately reuniting with his nephew and reclaiming the precious gift of family.

However, the shadows of the past refused to relent. Zale, the nemesis who had haunted Dylan's nightmares, resurfaced, robbing him of his sister, Cordelia, and plunging him into profound despair.

Years later, when his nephew embarked on his own vengeful quest, Dylan was all too happy to help. Although he no longer possessed enough courage to embark on a dangerous mission himself, he armed his nephew with both weapons and advice. The two are more similar than either care to admit.

When the triumphant return of his nephew, Gal, heralded a new era for Atlantis, Dylan made a solemn vow. He resolved to relinquish his reliance on alcohol, determined to seize the opportunity to reclaim his life from the clutches of darkness. Today, he resides in Atlantis, where he remains manager of the bar and ear to those in need, a testament to his resilience and the enduring spirit of a merman who emerged from the depths of despair to find purpose once more.

Raina Marsh

Raina Marsh emerged as the first offspring of Samantha Blue, the result of a union forged under somber circumstances. Wrought with apprehension about the consequences of birthing a descendant amidst the perils of predatory assaults, Samantha, in a moment of distress, opted to relinquish Raina for adoption. The aim was to place Raina in a landlocked environment, shielding her from the foreboding destiny woven into her mermaid lineage.

Raised by an adoptive mother with an aversion to water, Raina shied away from the ocean's embrace until the aftermath of the cataclysmic nuclear war. Surviving the devastating blasts, an instinctual pull led Raina to the coastline, where she immersed herself in the rejuvenating embrace of the sea. To her astonishment, the saltwater not only revitalized her weary form but unfurled her concealed mermaid tail. Battling exhaustion and radiation poisoning, she navigated her way to the island of Atlantis, guided by an innate connection.

Within Atlantis' mystical confines, Raina found solace in the healing waters of the Fountain of Youth, reuniting with her estranged mother, and discovering newfound kinship with half-siblings Cordelia and Dylan. Choosing to establish roots in Atlantis, Raina became entwined in a romantic alliance with Blaze, the last of the dragon kings. Their union bore fruit in the form of Ember, a testament to the harmonious convergence of their extraordinary lineages.

Devoting herself to family and community, Raina assumed the mantle of journalistic and reporting responsibilities on the enchanted island. As the guardian of Atlantis' tales and events, she not only safeguarded her lineage but also solidified her place as a cherished member of the legendary oceanic realm.

Ember

Ember stands as the last heir to the lineage of dragon kings, born of the union between Blaze and Raina. Unlike his majestic forebears, Ember grapples with the challenge of manifesting the renowned fiery breath that defines dragon kings. To compensate for this apparent shortcoming, he weaves a tapestry of humor and sarcasm, and turns to medicinal forms of cannabis to ease his emotional burdens.

However, Ember's fate took a captivating turn when he embarked on a quest to aid his best friend and cousin, Gal, in confronting an ancient adversary. During the odyssey, Ember unveiled a profound revelation—his inability to breathe fire is not a limitation, but his power manifested in the ability to inhale it instead.

Upon returning to Atlantis, Ember found himself adrift, still seeking his purpose on the island. Little does he know, a destiny of great significance awaits him as the chosen guardian of the revered orb of Fire and Heat. Currently cradled by his father and once held by the illustrious Cordelia Blue, this mystical artifact binds Ember to a legacy beyond his comprehension.

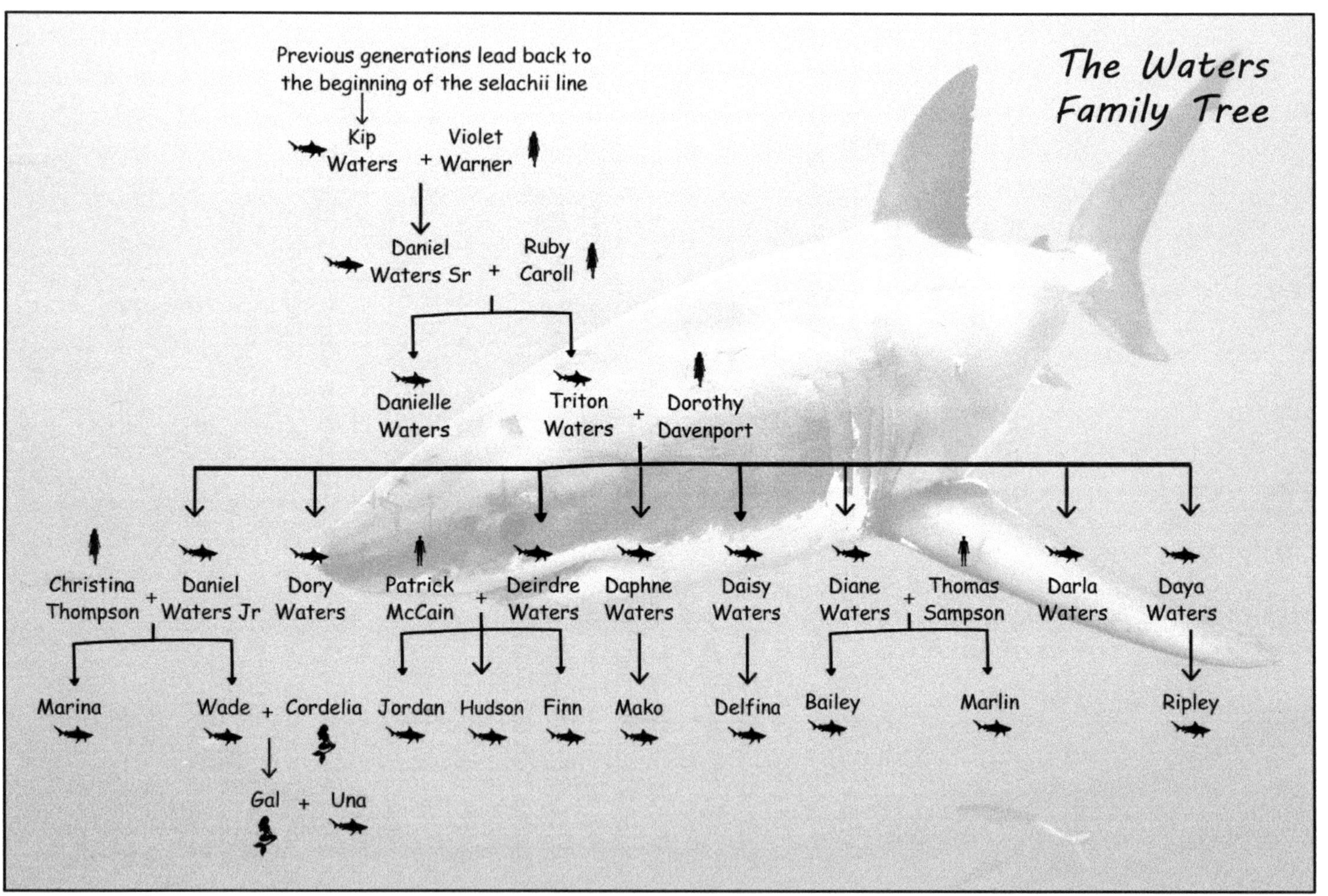
The Waters Family Tree
Previous generations lead back to the beginning of the selachii line
Kip Waters + Violet Warner
Daniel Waters Sr + Ruby Caroll
Danielle Waters
Triton Waters + Dorothy Davenport
Christina Thompson + Daniel Waters Jr
Dory Waters
Patrick McCain + Deirdre Waters
Daphne Waters
Daisy Waters
Diane Waters + Thomas Sampson
Darla Waters
Daya Waters
Marina
Wade + Cordelia
Jordan
Hudson
Finn
Mako
Delfina
Bailey
Marlin
Ripley
Gal + Una

Daniel Waters

Daniel emerged as the lone male heir among eight siblings, burdened with the legacy of Atlantis. His parents, fervent believers in the rightful dominion of selachii over land and sea, were determined to shatter the curse that had confined their kind to the watery depths.

Yet, Daniel, unlike his predecessors, harbored no aspirations for leadership. His heart belonged to the boundless expanse of the ocean, where he sailed aboard his fishing vessel alongside a steadfast crew of selachii sympathizers. With uncanny mastery, he employed his shapeshifting kin to aid in his fishing pursuits, earning him renown along the western shores as the most adept fisherman.

His prolonged absences necessitated the appointment of a guardian in the waters, a role unknowingly entrusted to Zale. Little did he fathom Zale's sinister motives; when Daniel's beloved wife was transformed into a selachii and imprisoned beneath the waves, he took matters into his own hands. For three years, he delved into the enigma of the pearl, enlisting the aid of his offspring, Marina and Wade, and their cousins. Despite relentless efforts, the secrets of the mysterious orb eluded him, plunging him into despair.

Upon the eventual liberation from the curse, Daniel rejoiced at the reunion with his wife, yet foresaw challenges arising from the union between his son and a mermaid. He cautioned against the divisive rifts it might sow among their kind, a warning heeded but not fully embraced by his son.

In the wake of Atlantis's rediscovery, Daniel chose the embrace of the open sea, drifting apart from his family. Mourning the loss of his wife, who met her fate battling the fearsome Hound of the Ocean, he lingered on the waters, a solitary sentinel. Although

reticent and reserved, he reserves a special affection for his grandson, Gal, and aided him in his quest to vanquish Zale.

Despite his advancing age, Daniel's spirit remains unyielding, his resolve unbroken. He stays adrift, tethered to the sea, haunted by the specter of the murderous selachii, yet still willing to lend his wisdom to the brave souls who venture forth into the unknown depths of their shared realm.

Christina Waters

Christina Waters, a devoted mother to Wade and beloved wife of Daniel, originally hailed from the world of humans. Her life took a turn when love blossomed with Daniel, who unveiled the enigmatic heritage of the selachii to her. Entranced by this revelation, Christina became immersed in the secrets of ocean shifters.

When she fell victim to a drowning event, a selachii resuscitation ritual saved her, transforming her into a shark shapeshifter. Yet, an ominous curse confined her beneath the waves until its bonds could be shattered.

For three long years, Zale held her captive, manipulating Daniel with dire threats to thwart any rescue attempts. It fell upon the shoulders of her children, Wade and Marina, to uncover the truth and liberate their mother while simultaneously breaking the curse.

The union of Cordelia and Wade proved instrumental in breaking the curse, allowing Christina to return home, regaining her transformative legs. However, wariness lingered within her as she observed the relationship between her son and his girlfriend.

Fearing the potential turmoil arising from a union between a selachii and a mermaid, Christina urged Wade's former flame and Marina's best friend, Stephanie, to rekindle her connection with Wade.

It was only after Stephanie's rejection by Wade and her subsequent transformation into a sea witch that Christina recognized her misguided judgment. She offered sincere apologies to her son and his new wife, finally embracing and supporting their union. Although she remained in the background of their relationship and life in Atlantis, her acceptance came with a heavy heart.

Tragedy struck with the arrival of the Hound of the Ocean, leading to Christina's untimely demise.

Wade Waters

Despite being the youngest among ten cousins, Wade bore the birthright to rule Atlantis, a birthright that would only come to fruition if Atlantis could be found.

From a tender age, Wade was immersed in the rich tapestry of selachii heritage. He embraced his ocean shifter lineage, learning to harness his extraordinary abilities. At the impressionable age of thirteen, his heart was forever captured by the enchanting Cordelia Blue, a mermaid of ancient lineage, though he remained blissfully unaware of her ancestry.

Intrigue and adventure soon swept Wade into a turbulent journey. A disastrous relationship with his sister's best friend, Stephanie, and the abduction of his mother by the selachii imposter, Zale, compelled Wade and his family to return to their ancestral home in San Diego. There, Wade's deepest desire was to rekindle his love for Cordelia, even if it meant keeping his selachii heritage a secret, for fear of scaring her away.

Fate had other plans in store when the merfolk, in a daring move, stole a magical white pearl from the grasp of the selachii. This act thrust Wade and his family into a quest to reclaim the pearl and unite their people. Unveiling Cordelia's true identity as the guardian of the stolen pearl tested Wade's love, but he remained steadfast in his devotion, even when she falsely accused him of betrayal.

As Wade delved deeper into the mysteries of the selachii leadership and Zale's malevolent intentions, he found himself on the side of truth, standing alongside the merfolk. Together, they harnessed the pearl's magic, restoring their ability to shift between sea and land, and were entrusted with the monumental task of locating the elusive Atlantis.

Amidst the trials and tribulations, Wade's heart never wavered from Cordelia, despite opposition from his parents and his own moments of doubt. His brief dalliance with his ex, Stephanie, made him realize that his heart belonged solely to Cordelia, even if the world was against their love.

Their journey to uncover the keys to open the portal to Atlantis was a testament to their love's resilience. United, they led their people through the portal to face the dragon kings. Wade even compelled his mother to apologize to Cordelia and promptly proposed to her, sealing their love in matrimony.

The joy of their union was marred as they learned of a devastating nuclear war on the mainland, blamed on the ocean shifters. Determined to help the surviving humans and provide closure for their people, Wade and Cordelia opened the gates to Atlantis, allowing humans sanctuary. However, a mercenary sought to punish Wade, leading to his capture. It took a concerted effort from his new wife, a friendly dragon king, and a united ocean shifter community to free him.

Upon their return to Atlantis, another formidable challenge awaited. Wade's spurned ex, Stephanie, had formed an alliance with the sea witch Aquaria, invoking the dreaded Hound of the Ocean. Only by uniting with a human named Babette did the three races overcome their adversities, albeit at a heartbreaking cost—Wade's mother perished on the shores of San Diego.

Several years of peace followed in Atlantis, with Wade and Cordelia ruling the island and making improvements for their people. However, the arrival of ghost pirates, who kidnapped their son, Gal, threw their world into turmoil. Witnessing Cordelia's mental health spiral was as painful as the fear for their son's fate, and Wade struggled to find a way to ease her burdens.

With unwavering love and determination, Wade and Cordelia defeated the ghost pirates, and their friends rallied by their side. But in the midst of their joyous reunion, the shadow of Zale, Wade's oldest enemy, cast darkness upon their lives, as he cruelly took Cordelia from him, leaving Wade completely broken.

Bereft of his beloved wife, Wade retreated into a numb existence, unable to parent or find purpose. His life held no meaning without Cordelia. It wasn't until his son, Gal, set out to confront Zale, that Wade realized the need to rebuild their relationship, for Cordelia would want them to remain close. The selachii monarchy was disbanded, and a democratic government took its place, though the people's loyalty to Wade and his son remained unwavering.

In time, Wade and Gal found solace in one another, easing the burden of their shared loss. Though their relationship was marked by trials, their enduring bond, along with the memory of Cordelia's love, served as a guiding light.

Marina Waters

Marina Waters, hailing from the esteemed lineage of selachii, is the elder sibling to Wade Waters and the firstborn child of Daniel and Christina. Despite the historical tension between merfolk and her own race, she has always harbored a profound sympathy for the merfolk.

When her brother became entwined in a profound love affair with a member of the merfolk community, Marina stood by their union, even if it meant betraying her closest friend. She envisioned this connection as a potential catalyst for fostering harmony among the ocean shifters.

Marina emerged as a prominent figure in the relentless pursuit to lift the curse that confined ocean shifters to the depths, guiding endeavors such as the quest for Atlantis, the confrontation with the Hound of the Ocean, and the clash against the sea witch, Stephanie—a once cherished friend. Since calling Atlantis home, Marina has attained revered status in the senate, contributing to the governance of the island and advocating for the diverse needs of ocean shifters.

Presently unattached and without heirs, Marina, under the mentorship of Dr. Christopher Blue, has assumed the role of a marine biologist. She diligently documents and seeks to understand the vibrant sea life surrounding Atlantis, contributing to the collective knowledge of her people.

Gal Waters

Gal Waters, only child of Wade and Cordelia, was born doubly into the royal line. From his earliest days, destiny had woven a complex tapestry around him. The tragic loss of his mother at a tender age thrust him on a difficult journey, one that would define his existence.

During a perilous encounter with ghost pirates, Gal showcased unparalleled resilience. He became the cornerstone that held the Atlantean children together, igniting their fading hope and inspiring them to defy despair. It was then that he unearthed his true purpose as the guardian of the orb of Snow & Ice, a role that bound him to the elemental forces of the frigid expanses. Despite the orb's waning power after the fierce battle against the ghost pirates, Gal felt an enduring connection to the icy realms, a connection that mirrored the quiet strength within him.

Gal was fated to ascend the throne as the Prince of Atlantis, destined to lead his people into the future. However, the shadows of his mother's tragic demise cast a pall over his heart. Fearful of the cruel hands of fate, he withdrew from the warmth of love and companionship, retreating into a solitary existence. The scars of loss etched deep, pushing him into a life haunted by resentment and dread, a life that saw him obliterate The Mermaid Chronicles in a desperate bid to escape the ominous prophecies.

His solitary journey took an unexpected turn when he embarked on a vengeful mission against Zale, the perpetrator of his mother's fate. In this pursuit, fate intertwined his destiny with Una and

Ember, two steadfast companions who refused to be left behind. Reluctantly burdened with their safety, Gal's icy exterior began to thaw in the face of genuine friendship and love. Una, with her unwavering spirit, breached the walls around his heart, teaching him the transformative power of human connection. Yet, the specter of loss continued to haunt him, a fear he confronted alongside Una, battling his inner demons and PTSD together.

In the depths of his journey, Gal unearthed the mythical Trident of Atlantis, proving himself worthy of its formidable power. With it, he vanquished Zale, seeking justice for his mother's untimely end. Upon his return to Atlantis, Gal immersed the trident in the Fountain of Youth, a gesture that not only rejuvenated the mystical waters but also resurrected The Mermaid Chronicles, ensuring their legacy lived on. The fountain's newfound accessibility to humans forged an unprecedented alliance between two worlds, bridging the gap between land and sea.

Gal, humbled by his past actions, extended a heartfelt apology to his people, who welcomed him back with open arms. Rejecting the notion of solitary leadership and dismissing the constraints of a traditional royal lineage, he proposed a progressive form of governance. The Atlanteans embraced this vision, heralding a new era where equality and unity reigned supreme. Despite his reservations, Gal's people continued to revere him as their prince, a title he wore with a newfound acceptance, forever tethered to their love and respect.

Although still fearful of the prophecies, Gal has accepted that there will be more adventures and ordeals to face.

Una Summers

Una Summers was born the eldest daughter of Trent and Maya. As she celebrated her fifth birthday, an ominous chapter unfurled when she was ensnared in a treacherous battle against ghostly pirates, becoming an unwitting captive aboard their nefarious vessel.

For fourteen harrowing days, Una endured the draining of her innocence, finding solace only in the companionship of her steadfast friends, Gal and Ember. Amidst her captivity, elemental orbs hidden beneath the city of Atlantis were unleashed. Upon the ship's return to the island, Una discovered her role as the guardian of the orb of Spirit and Soul. With newfound purpose, she guided her orb to unite with others, transforming the ghostly pirates into mortal beings and allowing the Atlanteans to defeat them.

Deeply rooted in her family's legacy, Una revered her ancestry, anticipating the day when she would ascend to the esteemed position of the Oracle of Atlantis, able to read and interpret the prophecies within The Mermaid Chronicles.

Taking after the courageous spirit of her parents, Una embarked on a daring quest to support her dear friend Gal in his mission to avenge his mother's tragic demise. Their journey spanned the globe, forging unbreakable bonds between the trio of valiant heroes. Amidst their odyssey, Una gently illuminated the depths of love to Gal, teaching him that affection was a force to be embraced. In time, he reciprocated her feelings, and their hearts entwined.

Empowered by her mystical orb, Una played an important role in the final battle against Zale. With unwavering determination, she aided her comrades, ensuring the victory of good over evil. After their triumph, Una, Gal, and Ember returned to Atlantis, where Gal and Una's relationship continues to flourish. She dutifully protects her magical purple orb, bestowing tranquility and empathy upon all who cross her path.

Zale Sefu

As previously stated, Zale became a selachii when he was targeted by high-school bullies and thrown into the ocean, unable to swim. When he was saved by the resuscitation ritual, Zale found a new home beneath the waves, although he nursed a burning desire for revenge for those responsible for his human death. Only if he could get his legs back would he be able to pursue his bullies and exact justice. His fury did not lesson over the years, even as his bullies became aged and decrepit, but instead his focus changed.

During his time beneath the waves Zale learned the selachii history and how much power could be his if he could only find the source of the rumored mystical artifacts. This led him to hunt for the pearl that could break the curse trapping him in the ocean and enable the selachii to transform to legs once more. His belief that only one race of ocean shifter species could use the pearl was erroneous, but also fueled his desire that he be the one to find it. To increase his chances, he attacked humans in the water to turn them into selachii and build the army he needed to find and retain the pearl.

Discovering the existence of the oldest line of merfolk and that they might possess the keys he so desired, he set his eyes on Samantha Blue and her children in order to steal the keys he believed they possessed. But the attack went wrong. Samantha Blue escaped to Atlantis, Dylan Blue was resuscitated by the merfolk, and he didn't get close to Cordelia.

Zale bid his time and was rewarded with the ownership of the pearl for a brief period, but he had no idea how to access its power. When the merfolk stole the pearl from his grasp, Zale swore vengeance on all of them, especially the young Cordelia Blue who was hinted at in a prophecy that she would be his end.

Attacking her friends and family, blackmailing her lover, and putting his army of selachii on her tail still did not bring him the results he desired. Wade and Cordelia used the pearl and managed to break the curse for all the ocean shifters, but Zale and

his trusty second in command, Caol, were punished by the High Council member, Gal. Imprisoned in a whirlpool with ashrays who bit them nightly, Zale and Caol spent several long years until they found a way to escape. With the death of all the original High Council members, the prison magic was weakened and Zale and Caol found a way out.

Going their separate ways, Zale sought refuse in the deepest parts of the ocean, seeking the dark gods of the old—The Denizens of the Deep. There he proved himself worthy and was granted megalodon size, his human

legs, as well as an enchanted rock that would blind the oracle in Atlantis and cloak his nefarious return.

Before returning to Atlantis for his final reckoning, Zale guided the ghost pirates to the island to steal Cordelia and Wade's child. He wanted to inflict the same pain they had imposed on him. To take what they most loved away. During the chaos of a battle with the ghost pirates, Zale made his presence known on the island. Seeing that Gal Waters had been rescued, Zale set his eyes on the seven-year-old child and attacked.

But Cordelia got to him first. Fearing this would be the moment the prophecy became true, Zale acted without mercy and closed his massive jaws around Cordelia, killing her, but also taking many unhealable wounds from her destructive fiery power.

Knowing the island wouldn't stand for the death of their beloved queen, Zale made an escape and took refuge in the northern waters. It wasn't until years later that he heard of Gal's quest for revenge. Knowing the battle would never be over until the entire Waters line was wiped out, Zale prepared to kill Gal.

During the journey, Zale learned that Vorago's trident was indeed real and held an unfathomable power. Changing his plans to track Gal until he found the trident, he planned to kill him after the magical artifact was in his possession. But his schemes did not pan out. After Gal secured the trident and Zale confronted him, he was met with an unexpected and immense power. Although he fought hard for everything he believed he deserved, the power of the trident in Gal's hand was too much, and the revenge in Gal's heart too strong. Zale succumbed to his wounds.

Caol Ortega

Caol was a renowned diver among humans, fearless in his pursuit of the mysteries hidden beneath the waves. His extraordinary abilities and unyielding curiosity led him to explore the farthest reaches of the Earth's oceans, unveiling secrets that remained hidden from ordinary eyes.

However, Caol's human journey took an unexpected turn when he faced a perilous underwater accident. Out of air, he lay trapped on the ocean floor. As the cold currents threatened to claim him, a group of selachii came to his aid. Recognizing the potential within him, they performed the resuscitation ritual, and transformed him into one of their own.

Among the selachii, Caol forged a fast friendship with a fellow shapeshifter named Zale. Desperate to return to his family, he joined Zale on a mission to hunt for the mystical pearl, knowing that breaking the curse was the only way he could return to land. The duo, possessing a captivating charm, became inseparable, leaving an indelible mark on underwater folklore. Zale's dark and enigmatic aura complemented Caol's adventurous spirit.

Under Zale's influence, Caol's motives grew darker, driven by the belief that they could rule the oceans if they could only break the curse. However, their plans went awry, resulting in their imprisonment. Caol blamed Zale for his imprisoned predicament, and vowed vengeance on Cordelia Blue.

After escaping a prison whirlpool, Caol reached Atlantis, where he drank from the Fountain of Youth and regained his legs. Determined to seize power, he stole a magical orb needed to defeat ghost pirates and held it ransom, relishing the pain on Cordelia's face.

But Cordelia too had changed. She had become fiercely protective of her family, and Caol didn't count on her attacking him while he still possessed the orb. This vast misjudgment led to his untimely death.

Aquaria

Aquaria, a mermaid of extraordinary beauty, once reveled in the embrace of her fellow merfolk. Bound to the sea, she longed for the forbidden lands above, where her tail would transform into legs. The charismatic High Council member, Gal, captivated by her allure, dared to bridge the gap between their worlds. Their passionate union birthed Blaze, a dragon king destined for greatness. Yet, Gal's duties kept him tethered to the Council's chamber, and Aquaria's heart darkened with envy.

Fueled by jealousy, she delved into the forbidden arts, evolving into a formidable sea witch, following her sister's dark path. Together, as scorned women, they summoned the Hound of the Sea to wreak havoc upon ocean shifters, driven by Aquaria's desire for Gal's attention. In a brutal battle, her sister fell, and the hound was subdued, but Aquaria's wrath endured.

Nursing her wounds, Aquaria's heart turned to stone, her rage fixated on Gal and her son, Blaze, who had abandoned her. Years passed, and during a fateful encounter with Cordelia, seeking Atlantis, Aquaria's heart wrenched at the sight of Gal, rekindling her vendetta. Vowing vengeance, she unleashed her serpentine minions upon the unsuspecting group, but was unsuccessful in her desires.

A year later, an opportunity materialized as Stephanie, now a fellow sea witch, allied with Aquaria, seeking her dark wisdom. Together, they invoked the hound once more, intending to obliterate the ocean shifters and exact revenge. Unbeknownst to Aquaria, a powerful alliance stood against her, and it was Blaze, repulsed by her choices, who ended her wretched existence, putting an end to her legacy of bitterness and wrath.

Stephanie

Stephanie Bowers, an adventurous and curious human, had her destiny forever altered when she crossed paths with Marina Waters. Little did Stephanie know that this encounter would plunge her into a world of selachii, where the secrets of the ocean's depths held both peril and fascination.

Marina Waters, a selachii of ancient lineage, captivated Stephanie with tales of her family's heritage. As Stephanie delved deeper into the world of ocean shifters, she couldn't help but be drawn to Marina's younger brother, Wade. Their passionate love affair was brief but intense, an unforgettable connection that left a lasting mark on her heart.

However, it wasn't until after their romance had run its course that Stephanie realized the depth of her feelings for Wade. She yearned for a second chance, a rekindling of the flames that once burned so brightly between them. Determined to win him back, she was willing to go to great lengths.

Tragedy struck one fateful day when Stephanie found herself unable to leave the water. She had been transformed into a selachii, forever bound to the ocean's depths. Yet, her determination to be with Wade persisted. She longed for a way to return to the land and be reunited with him.

The key to her salvation came through Wade and Cordelia, who together broke the curse that had imprisoned Stephanie beneath the waves. As best friends with Marina, Stephanie seized the opportunity to insert herself into the quest to find Atlantis, hoping to not only uncover its secrets but also to win Wade's heart once more.

With Wade's mother on her side, Stephanie employed every artful strategy in her arsenal to regain Wade's affection. She secured his heart with a kiss and enlisted his parents' insistence that he be with a fellow selachii. Yet, the path to love was fraught with obstacles. Cordelia's presence continually vied for Wade's attention, and Stephanie found herself embroiled in a losing battle for his affections.

Wade's declaration that he could never love her as he did Cordelia was a painful blow to Stephanie's heart. She withdrew, nursing her wounds and grappling with rejection. Resilient and determined, Stephanie had never been one to accept failure. A simmering resentment began to take root within her.

Seeking solace in the arms of Wade's cousin, Jordan, Stephanie had no intention of commitment. Instead, she used the time to plan her revenge.

As Stephanie's obsession grew, she embarked on a treacherous path toward becoming a sea witch, determined to unleash chaos and destruction upon Atlantis. She delved into the dark arts, learning forbidden incantations from Aquaria. Her ultimate goal was to summon the fearsome Hound of the Ocean, hoping it would wreak havoc on the ocean shifters and their precious island. Her descent into darkness was complete.

However, Stephanie's plans went awry, and her attempts to destroy Atlantis were thwarted when the hound and Aquaria were killed.

Consumed by her quest for revenge, Stephanie unleashed her venomous snakes upon Atlantis, inflicting as much harm as she could.

It was Jordan, his heart heavy with the pain of a love lost, who confronted Stephanie in her malevolent transformation. With a swift act, he brought about her end with a blade to her chest.

The tragic tale of Stephanie Bowers will forever serve as a cautionary legend among the merfolk, a reminder of the devastating consequences that can result from unchecked vengeance and obsession in the depths of the ocean

Trent Summers

Born amidst the gentle whispers of San Diego's coastal winds, Trent was an only child destined for extraordinary fortunes beneath the waves. Academia was not his forte, but in the realms of both surfing and acting, he found his true calling. His talent adorned Disney movies, and his prowess on the waves garnered sponsorship from Quicksilver, marking him as a legend in both worlds.

Trent's potential was cut short when Caol transformed him into a fellow shark shapeshifter during a fateful surf competition. Bound by the curse, with no remedy yet in sight from Cordelia and Wade, Trent was severed from the familiar shores and faces of his past. Trent regained the use of his legs mere weeks later, an astonishing phenomenon that rekindled the joy of reunion with his parents. However, this moment of family unity was but a brief respite in the face of impending calamity, for both parents perished in the nuclear war.

Trent fell in love with Maya Galaris during the quest for the jewels that would transport them to Atlantis. Reluctant for her to become a mermaid, having lived the trials of being an ocean shifter, Trent was nonetheless supportive when the transformation saved her life. Their love story culminated in a sacred union in Atlantis, where they nurtured a family of four precious children.

In Atlantis, Trent channeled his passion for surfing into teaching, guiding aspiring shapeshifters in the art of riding the ocean's rhythms. Additionally, he pioneered a media company to bring film and movies to the island. He is also a member of the senate, but claims that his most important role is "being the man behind the woman."

Angelica

Angelica, revered leader of the dwindling orcanian populace, masters of orca shapeshifting who traverse the icy depths of the Antarctic seas, holds a tale woven with the currents of fate and redemption. Her clan, a reclusive kin, cloistered within their frozen realm, distanced themselves from the affairs of other ocean shifters and the politics entwined in Atlantis's depths.

Tragedy unfurled its dark tendrils when her nephew, Frost, faced the brink of demise, injured in a ruthless assault by ashrays driven to desperation after the disappearance of their usual prey—the selachii. Faced with the direst of circumstances, Angelica turned to Zale, her enigmatic confidant, unaware of his shadowed past. Entrusting his counsel, she embarked on a journey to the Fountain of Youth within Atlantis, the sole beacon of hope for Frost's salvation. As a token of gratitude to Zale, and at his request, she cast a mysterious black stone into the glistening waters of the fountain.

Blinded by desperation and trust, Angelica unwittingly plunged Atlantis into chaos, shrouding Maya's visions and the prophecies within this very book. When the ghost pirates attacked and Zale was revealed to be the master behind the chaos, Angelica was overwhelmed by remorse. With contrition heavy in her heart, she confided her sins to Cordelia, and with her guidance, she retrieved the blinding stone, restoring clarity to Maya's visions and the prophecies entwined within The Mermaid Chronicles.

With newfound purpose, Angelica pledged herself and her clan on the quest to recover the elemental orbs and combat the ghost pirates, bringing her to a harrowing confrontation with the dreaded Caol, where she almost lost her life.

As the echoes of battle faded and the sea mourned Cordelia's passing, Angelica resolved that her clan must depart Atlantis, returning to the frigid embrace of Antarctica's icy depths. Still mourning her part in Cordelia's passing, Angelica was determined to help the young Gal Waters in his quest to seek vengeance. She and her clan remain in Antarctica.

High Council Members

Esmerelda

When the legendary island of Atlantis succumbed to the dominion of the dragon kings, Esmerelda emerged as the esteemed High Council representative of the merfolk. Possessing an extraordinary blend of foresight and mystical prowess, she orchestrated the creation of the resplendent blue chamber, a sanctuary crafted for herself and her fellow counselors to seek refuge in the aftermath of Atlantis's fall. Over centuries, cocooned within the nebulous walls of the blue chamber, they protected the Power of the Sea, patiently awaiting the opportune moment when their sunken island would be rediscovered.

Esmerelda, though not the most physically demonstrative or affectionate, possessed unparalleled wisdom, encompassing the intricate history of shapeshifting beings. Her knowledge of the shifting sands of time was profound. Firm in her teachings, she tolerated no fools and needed no second requests. Her guidance was reserved for those merfolk who displayed initiative, yet she occasionally clung to the traditional ways of Atlantis, resisting the tide of change that swept through their world.

The mermaid emissary compelled her fellow counselors to persevere and steadfastly reminding them of their sacred duties to Atlantis. A paragon of true leadership, she wielded her authority with a measured severity, ensuring that hope endured even in the darkest depths of uncertainty. Though confined to the blue chamber for eons, Esmerelda extended her influence beyond, occasionally offering a guiding hand to merfolk dwelling in the human realm. One such instance saw her nudging The Mermaid Chronicles into the hands of Maya, an act that rippled through the tides of destiny.

Little did Cordelia realize that Esmerelda was an unseen ancestor whose influence subtly shaped the currents of her existence.

Esmerelda gave her life helping Cordelia during the batter with the Hound of the Ocean and the sea witches Aquaria and Stephanie.

Esmerelda was not one to forgive easily, and she seldom saw fault in her own actions. However, once she stood by your side, her loyalty was unwavering, making her a steadfast and trusted companion in the mesmerizing depths of the oceanic realm

Shane

Shane stood as the esteemed selachii representative on the High Council. Following the tragic fall of Atlantis at the hands of the dragon kings, he chose the solace of the revered blue chamber. Unlike his counterpart, Gal, who ventured into the human realm despite the toll of accelerated aging, Shane remained aloof from the affairs of the ocean shifters.

Haunted by the shame that the selachii had failed to safeguard Atlantis from the dragon king onslaught, and witnessing the malevolent machinations of Zale and Caol in their pursuit of the Power of the Sea, Shane withdrew into the shadows within the blue chamber for many years. He patiently awaited the day when the honor of the selachii would be restored. Finally realizing he had to take matters into his own hands, Shane fervently advocated for his fellow selachii, tirelessly pleading with the formidable mermaid emissary, Esmerelda. He argued against the unjust punishment of the ashrays. Though his pleas fell on deaf ears, he persisted, unyielding in his belief in unity among all aquatic beings.

In the face of Esmerelda's obstinacy, Shane, burdened but undeterred, retreated into the shadows of the council's decisions, his voice subdued. It was a silent vigil he maintained until the fateful day when Cordelia Blue and Wade Waters, brave souls with hearts as vast as the ocean, arrived in the blue chamber. With newfound determination, Shane arose from his quietude, demanding that Esmerelda heed their plight and restore their lost freedom.

Yet, fate wove a tragic thread into Shane's story. In the throes of a battle against the formidable Hound of the Ocean, when human mercenaries invaded Atlantis, Shane sacrificed his life. In his final moments, he entrusted the guardianship of the Power of the Sea to Babette, a human. It was a selfless act, driven by the hope that this gesture would foster unity among all races for generations to come.

Edward

Edward stood as the final guardian of the eelusionists, a unique lineage of shapeshifters who could seamlessly morph into electric eels, wielding their formidable powers of electricity in the art of defensive warfare. These elusive beings, skilled not only in physical prowess but also in the craft of illusion, were an exceedingly rare breed among the ocean shifters.

Once, a clan of eel shifters thrived alongside him, but they vanished like whispers in the current when the dragon kings laid siege to Atlantis. Edward narrowly escaped, seeking refuge in the sanctuary of the blue chamber. Throughout the centuries spent within the hallowed confines of the chamber, Edward maintained a tranquil demeanor. Known for his reserved nature, he navigated the discussions and debates with fellow counselors without ever succumbing to temper. His keen observational skills allowed him to prepare for the gradual decline of ocean shifters in the human realm, a fate that deeply concerned him.

His once-mastered art of transforming into an eel and conversing fluently with every eel species was overshadowed by a deep solitude, and was unable to help Cordelia Blue and her companions when they faced a perilous encounter with electric eels.

When the ominous Hound of the Ocean threatened the ocean shifters, Edward emerged from the blue chamber. In a pivotal moment, he ventured beyond its confines to deliver a vital portion of the Power of the Sea to Cordelia and Wade, aiding them in their courageous battle against the colossal sea creature.

Yet, as the eldest member of the esteemed High Council, Edward lingered outside the protective sanctuary longer than advisable. Time, relentless as the tides, swiftly caught up with him, and he succumbed to the inevitability of aging just as the triumphant conclusion of the battle unfolded. In his final moments, Edward's legacy resonated through the victorious echoes of the oceanic saga, forever etching his name among the mythical heroes of the underwater realm.

Gal

Gal, the youngest member of the High Council, was the dragon king representative. Tradition dictated the presence of a dragon king on the council, and when his brethren seized Atlantis from the merfolk and selachii, he was appalled by their actions. Choosing to disassociate from his own kind, Gal aligned himself with fellow counselors in the sanctity of the blue chamber.

Behind his fierce exterior, Gal possessed a heart as vast as the ocean, ever willing to extend a helping hand to strangers, embodying kindness in its purest form. Gal's compassion and courage knew no bounds. In the initial years, Gal tirelessly ventured outside the chamber, attempting to negotiate with the dragon kings to reclaim Atlantis for the merfolk. When labeled a traitor and met with deaf ears, he reluctantly retreated to the confines of the chamber. However, fate intervened when a captivating mermaid named Aquaria captured his attention. Once more, Gal found himself outside the chamber, eventually fathering a young dragon king.

Esmerelda reminded him of his responsibilities to all ocean shifters, urging him to focus on resolving their collective issues within the chamber. Gal, burdened by duty, left his son in the care of the mermaid Aquaria. Witnessing his cherished love succumb to bitterness, and then transform into a sea witch, saddened Gal profoundly. Vowing not to meddle in external affairs again, he immersed himself in the chamber's deliberations.

Throughout his millennia-long existence, Gal's life was adorned with remarkable facts. His age stretched over a thousand years, marking him as a living legend among merfolk. His favorite hue, a vibrant red, mirrored the fiery spirit within him. His fiery prowess was awe-inspiring; his fireballs could soar over 300 yards, reaching temperatures that could melt the very depths of the sea.

Fate took an unexpected turn with the arrival of Cordelia. Lost and imperiled by ice demons, Gal couldn't stand idly by. Despite his previous failures with his son, he intervened to save Cordelia's life. Filled with remorse for his past shortcomings, Gal embraced Cordelia as a surrogate daughter. During the pivotal battle to reclaim Atlantis, he willingly sacrificed his life for her, determined not to repeat the mistakes of his past.

Babette

Babette and Cordelia's destinies first intertwined during their formative years, where the pursuit of Wade's affections stirred the waters of their high-school existence.

Born and raised in the sun-kissed realms of California, Babette was no ordinary human. Her father, a venerable figure who managed FEMA and bore the weight of military wisdom, imparted upon her the art of weaponry, foreseeing a future where such skills would be imperative. During the chaos of a nuclear war, Babette and her father, survivors amidst the ruins of their family, establishing a sanctuary for refugees that unwittingly brought them face-to-face with a ruthless band of human mercenaries, as well as a compassionate hand to those plagued by injury and radiation sickness. It was here, during the trials of survival, that Babette's destiny intertwined with the merfolk and selachii.

As the turbulence between ocean shifters and humans escalated into open conflict, Babette emerged as an unexpected bridge between worlds. The moment of unity arrived when Babette harnessed the power of Cordelia's enchanted ring, shielding both ocean shifters and humans from the lethal breath of the monstrous hound. Following the battle, Babette found a home in Atlantis, engaging in an on-again, off-again relationship with Dylan Blue. Entrusted with the guardianship of the Power of the Sea and the only human able to use the Fountain of Youth, she navigated the skeptical gaze of her race.

The High Council, traditionally an assembly of shifter elders, welcomed her as the first human member. In a bid to unite the disparate races sharing the island, Babette played a pivotal role in rescuing numerous ocean shifters from the clutches of the human mercenaries. Her courageous confrontation with the dreaded Hound of the Ocean cemented her position as the human representative.

Haunted by a sense of responsibility, Babette dedicated herself to establishing a haven for those unable to access the fountain's rejuvenating waters. Discomforted by the curious scrutiny, she frequently embarked on months-long journeys to the mainland in search of survivors from the nuclear catastrophe.

Eventually, frustrated by the lack of progression of her relationship with Dylan and with the call of the open seas beckoning her, Babette sailed away from Atlantis, her departure marking the end of an era. However, fate had other plans as she became entangled in a new struggle, aiding Cordelia's son during a fierce Icelandic snowstorm. Bravely supporting Gal and his companions, Babette succumbed to the tempest, relinquishing her life. Her body was returned to Atlantis and she was celebrated in the traditional Atlantean way.

Blaze

Blaze was born of noble lineage, the offspring of the powerful dragon king, Gal, and the enchanting mermaid, Aquaria, before her transformation into a sea witch. While his father, a distinguished member of the High Council in the esteemed blue chamber, diligently fulfilled his duties, Blaze was nurtured in the depths of the ocean's kelp forests, solely under the guidance of his mermaid mother.

For a decade, he witnessed his mother's growing resentment toward his father, and her subsequent descent into the dark arts. Heartbroken by her tragic transformation, Blaze left his home despite her pleas, embarking on a quest for his own destiny and adventure.

In his wanderings, Blaze occasionally encountered his father, relishing the rare moments spent in the company of the heroic dragon king. Though he yearned for more paternal attention, Blaze understood the importance of Gal's obligations as a High Council member and vowed to live his life with honesty and bravery, mirroring his father's virtues.

During the turmoil of the nuclear war, Gal crossed paths with Cordelia Blue and Wade Waters. Blaze played a vital role in aiding Wade's escape from the clutches of a human mercenary, Sean Williams, alongside other ocean shifters. Using his fiery powers, Blaze contributed to the defeat of the dreaded Hound of the Ocean, forging alliances and friendships.

In the heat of battle, Blaze confronted his mother, recognizing the darkness that had consumed her. Realizing her heart had been consumed by bitterness and loveless despair, he reluctantly used his fiery breath to end her suffering.

Acknowledging his bravery and his status as the last dragon king, Blaze was bestowed a position on the High Council, a responsibility he was uncertain he desired. Within the hallowed halls of Atlantis, Blaze found solace in the company of Cordelia, who had shared a deep connection with his late father. Through her, he discovered facets of his father's character, learning to love her as deeply as he had loved his departed parent.

Gal's heart found its match in Raina, Cordelia's sister, resulting in the birth of a dragon king heir named Ember. Although their romantic union was fleeting, Blaze and Raina parted amicably, their hearts leading them in different directions. Blaze keeps the identity of the one who holds his heart's dominion a secret, cherishing the civility and friendship that transcends realms.

Blaze became the guardian of the orb of Fire & Heat after Cordelia's tragic death.

Ford

Ford's early years were guided by the wisdom of his parents, two selachii whose bloodline traced back to the royal guards of Atlantis. Their love and devotion instilled in Ford a sense of duty and honor, a legacy he cherished deeply. They regaled him with tales of the ancient curse that bound their kind to the depths, away from the intrigues and darkness that plagued the land-dwellers.

Yet, fate had grand plans for Ford, entwining his destiny with two extraordinary humans, Cordelia and Wade, whose love story transcended the boundaries of their worlds. Their arrival marked the breaking of the age-old curse that had kept the merfolk hidden beneath the waves. Ford observed the unfolding events from his remote enclave, marveling at the bravery and power displayed by the young lovers as they rediscovered Atlantis and defied the malevolent Zale.

Impressed by Cordelia and Wade's courage, Ford pledged his unwavering loyalty to them, vowing to be their committed bodyguard. His efforts were not in vain, for he had spent years honing his skills in various forms of underwater combat, and ensured that no harm would befall the royal couple under his watchful gaze. This oath extended to Gal Waters, the young prince born into their world, whom Ford cherished as if he were his own kin.

Tragedy struck when Gal was abducted by the ghostly pirates. Ford's heartache fueled his determination, leading him on a relentless quest to recover the young prince. In his pursuit of the elemental orbs, he discovered his role as the guardian of Earth and Rock.

With newfound abilities coursing through his veins, Ford confronted the ghost pirates, channeling the elemental forces of Earth and Rock to vanquish their spectral menace. The victory came at a great cost, for Cordelia was lost to the depths, leaving Ford to shoulder the burden of protecting her grieving family.

In the wake of Cordelia's passing, Ford redoubled his efforts, becoming a steadfast guardian to the reclusive king, Wade, and the young prince, Gal. Despite Wade's withdrawal from the world and Gal's reluctance to embrace his merfolk heritage, Ford remained committed to his role of guidance and protection. His days were spent patrolling the borders of Atlantis, his keen eyes ever watchful for signs of danger, his heart filled with the resolve to safeguard his newfound family.

Ford's loyalty extended not only to the royal lineage but also to the essence of Atlantis itself. He became a living testament to the enduring spirit of the ocean shifters, a symbol of their resilience and bravery in the face of adversity.

Maya

Maya Summers, born Maya Galaris, was left an orphan at birth when her parents valiantly assisted the merfolk in the inaugural clash against the formidable Hound of the Ocean. Throughout her formative years, she found solace in the company of a single foster family, where she shared her life with three younger foster siblings, none of whom survived the tumultuous waves of the nuclear war.

Years later, she emerged into the realm of ocean shifters, not as a shapeshifter, but as a human oracle deeply entwined with the mysteries of The Mermaid Chronicles. The lineage of this enchanting ability traced its way through generations of females, finding its ultimate resting place upon Maya's capable shoulders.

With the High Council confined to the blue chambers, Maya's destiny was gently guided toward Cordelia, where a profound friendship blossomed between them. Through subtle mystical encouragement, Maya unraveled The Mermaid Chronicles, validating her long-held instincts about the existence of merfolk. However, convincing her companions proved to be a formidable challenge until Cordelia discovered own mermaid tail.

Endowed with the unique ability to decipher the ancient prophecies within The Mermaid Chronicles, Maya assumed the role of a guiding light for her shapeshifting brethren, steering them through treacherous quests and moments of disquiet.

Maya's heart harbored an enduring desire to become a mermaid herself, and fate intervened on a momentous day during her quest for Atlantis. Faced with a life-threatening situation, Maya underwent the resuscitation ritual led by Dylan Blue, culminating in her transformation into a mermaid.

In the era when ocean shifters reclaimed their aquatic forms and Maya played an instrumental role in the rediscovery and reclamation of Atlantis, she found her haven on the island alongside her husband, Trent, and their four children. Maya remains the oracle, ever attuned to the whispers of the ocean and the enigmatic prophecies that shaped the destiny of her kin.

Yet, Maya's profound ability to decipher The Mermaid Chronicles and illuminate the prophecies was momentarily shrouded in darkness during a harrowing skirmish with ghostly pirates, when a member of the orcana concealed a blinding stone within the fountain. The stone was eventually unearthed, allowing Maya to reclaim her vision and understanding of the sacred prophecies.

Today, Maya stands resolute in her role as a devoted member of the High Council, ever the instrumental oracle, dedicated to unraveling the enigmatic prophecies and guiding the destiny of the realm's inhabitants with her unwavering insight.

PART FOUR

THE PROPHECIES

A sanctuary will form for the hunted

Known only to those with hearts pure as the clearest waters, a sanctuary will emerge as a beacon of hope for merfolk, selachii, orcana, and all other ocean shapeshifters who find themselves pursued by relentless foes.

The Tidal Covenant

When the three water gods, Vorago, Cascadia, and Tempest, join their powers in a sacred covenant, the ocean shall grant its chosen champions the ability to shapeshift at will, blurring the boundaries between land and sea.

The Divine Heir

Vorago's trident, a symbol of divine authority, will choose a worthy successor to guard the seas.

Coral Crown

Cascadia's coral crown holds the key to unlocking the ancient prophecies, written in the language of the deep.

Fire and Brimstone

Vorago's wrath shall cleanse the tainted waters, restoring balance to the realm.

Song of the Selachii

When the selachii's song is heard by all the sea creatures, it will signal a time of great transformation. Those who embrace their true nature will find strength beyond measure.

The Selkie's Choice

The selkie will face a choice that will determine the course of the oceans. To save their kin, they must choose between shedding their pelt forever or forsaking their people.

Mermaid Tears
Cascadia's tears, when offered to the Ocean's Heart,
can grant the most profound wishes of the faithful.

Pearls of Destiny
When the last pearl falls from the night sky,
a new pathway to Atlantis shall be paved.

Serpent's Riddle

The Eelusionists' hidden city is guarded by the Serpent's Riddle, a puzzle only the worthy can solve.

Watery Wounds

Mermaids' tears will heal the ocean's wounds, but only when united with the emotion of mortal hearts.

Secrets of Portals and Dreams

The orcana's future is in a lost realm beneath the seabed, accessible only through dreams.

Forbidden Love Strikes Misery

When the selachii queen's heart is stolen by a mortal, the fate of her kind hangs in the balance.

Shadows of the Sea

Beneath the crimson tide, the Eelusionists' dance shall unveil forgotten truths, hidden in the shadows of the sea.

A Call for Vigilance

Complacency shall breed malevolence. When the merfolk and selachii grow idle, the sinister forces of the deep shall seize the opportunity to sow chaos.

Whispers of the Sea

Mermaids' songs will enchant mortal sailors, guiding them safely through treacherous waters. But mortals must beware the power of their voices.

Starborn Hunt

When the starfish align in the constellation of the Leviathan, the selachii shall gather for a fateful hunt.

Tides of Unity

Merfolk and orcana must unite to protect the enchanted coral groves of their ancestors.

From Unseen Depths

The Eelusionists' leader will emerge from the Crystal Caves, bearing the responsibility of protecting the revealing squid ink.

Tears of the Deep

Mermaid tears, when mixed with the ink of an ancient prophecy, reveal the future of the ocean realm.

The Siren's Rescue

When the siren's song echoes through the coral caverns, it foretells a time of profound transformation. Those who heed her call will be saved from a drowning fate and resuscitated as a new being.

The Mariner's Compass

Within the heart of a humble mariner lies the compass that can guide the ocean shifters through their darkest trials. The lost shall find their way home.

Scales of the Tempest

Mermaid scales, coveted by treasure hunters, possess the power to calm storms or unleash tempests.

Veil of Illusions

The Eelusionists' greatest test lies in the Veil of Illusions, where truth and deception dance as one.

Crimson Stains of a Blood Moon

When the blood moon stains the ocean's surface, the selachii shall be drawn into a battle that determines their fate.

The Secrets of Shifting Tides

A mermaid of noble spirit shall undergo a profound metamorphosis, and she will become the guardian of ancient secrets.

The Shell of Wisdom
Vorago's wisdom flows through the sacred seashell,
Whispered to those who seek counsel from the sea.

Cascadia's Cradle

Cascadia's embrace will cradle lost souls, guiding them to the eternal depths of the Ocean's Keep.

The Birth of the Pearlborn

From the depths of the abyss, a pearlborn shall rise, born of both land and sea. They will possess the power to bridge the realms, bringing harmony or chaos depending on their choice.

A Tidal Reckoning

As half the royal line shall be diminished, in the tides of destiny, their fate is finished. The royal mermaid line, once numerous and resplendent, will find themselves teetering on the precipice of extinction, unless the remaining solitary heir faces her destiny.

The Twin's Legacy

Twins bound by love, torn by fate. As one seeks solace on land, the other drifts into the abyss. Yet in the heart of fear lies the seed of courage, and in the depths of grief blooms the flower of hope.

Tail of Destiny

Hope for ocean shifters springs anew as the royal one realizes her tail. With each graceful movement, this mermaid, touched by the ancient magic of the seas, will embody the hopes and dreams of her kind, becoming a beacon of change. Her realization of her true nature, her majestic tail, will herald a time of transformation and renewal, not only for herself but for the entire merfolk community.

Shattering the Curses of Destiny

The one who walks the land can break the curse, united. When a being who walks the land joins forces with another of the ocean, the shackles of curses that bind the underwater realms shall shatter. United in purpose and unwavering in determination, they shall unlock the secrets of their intertwined fates and unleash a new era.

Heart's Flame

The journey to the sunken land is filled with heartache and loss. The fire mermaid must be determined. To reach the fabled sunken land, one must tread a path fraught with heartache and loss. It is a journey that demands unwavering determination, especially from the fiery-hearted mermaid whose passion and courage will serve as a guiding light through the darkest abyss. Her determination shall fan the flames of hope and kindle the fires of renewal for the land long lost to the depths.

The Trinity Bond

To save Atlantis the royal couple must unite with a third, the one who died and lives again. Family is important. The royal couple, torn asunder by fate, must forge an unbreakable bond with a third, one who has tasted the bitter embrace of death and emerged anew. In their unity, they shall unearth the forgotten wisdom of their ancestors and discover that the strength of family, in both blood and spirit, is the key to unlocking the mysteries of their underwater realm.

Betrayal's Crucible: The Test of the Triad

The united three must battle ancient enemies in the face of great betrayal. Betrayal, like a treacherous undercurrent, will test their resolve. In the crucible of deceit, they must summon their deepest strengths, trust in one another, and confront the foes that have haunted their lineage for generations.

The Denizen's Awakening

Beneath the ocean's heart, the Denizens of the Deep stir to provide aid to a mighty selachii. Its awakening will herald a time of cataclysmic change, causing the fate of the royal line to hang in the balance.

The one who sees will not see

A pivotal figure, one gifted with insight and foresight, may be blind to the truth that unfolds before them. Even those with the

Ghostly Vengeance Seeks Innocence
Vengeful apparitions shall rise seeking
retribution against innocent souls of Atlantis.

The Trident Bearer's Duty

When the Leviathan stirs from its slumber, an unwilling merman must wield the trident to avert catastrophe.

greatest visions may be blinded by their own preconceptions, and the path to enlightenment may require looking beyond the surface to discover hidden truths.

Twilight's Deception

In the dance of shadows and light, trust becomes a fleeting wisp, elusive as the morning mist. Whispers of loyalty, echoes of deceit, as alliances waver and faith hangs by a thread.

Old enemies die hard

The echoes of long-standing enemies will resonate through the ages, refusing to be silenced.

Dawn of Deep Serenity

When the mermaid queen ascends to the Celestial Abyss, a new era of peace will dawn in the depths.

Sea Splitter: The Power of Vorago's Trident

Vorago's trident, when wielded by a true heart, can part the sea itself, revealing hidden paths.

Forge of Fury

Vorago's trident, reforged in the forge of a volcanic abyss, will become an instrument of divine justice.

Trident's Trials

The Denizens of the Deep crave the power of Vorago's trident. The one true wielder must remain strong.

ABOUT THE AUTHOR

Marisa Noelle is the author behind a treasure trove of middle-grade and young adult novels that dance through the realms of science-fiction, fantasy, horror, dystopian, and mental health. From unraveling mysteries to diving deep into the human psyche, she's your go-to wordsmith for adventures that'll tickle your imagination.

Marisa's literary exploits include "The Shadow Keepers," a spine-tingling tale to keep you up all night, and "The Unraveling of Luna Forester," a masterpiece that snagged the prestigious First Place Incipere Award, rocked the WriteBlend Finalist stage, waltzed as a BBYNA Semi-Finalist, and took its place on the Bookshelf Finalist shelf. With dystopian being one of her favorite genres, you can expect fast-paced thrills from the world of "The Unadjusteds Trilogy," a rollercoaster ride featuring "The Unadjusteds," "The Rise of the Altereds," and "The Reckoning," perfect for fans of

Divergent, Maze Runner & The Hunger Games. And don't forget to dive into "The Mermaid Chronicles," a series that will plunge you into the depths of "Secrets of the Deep," lead you on a wild "Quest for Atlantis," challenge you to "Fight for Freedom," send shivers down your spine with "Ghost Pirates," and leave you craving "Vendetta." She also writes steamy romance under the pen name Savannah Warner.

When Marisa's not weaving literary spells, she's helping mold the future of MG and YA authors as a mentor for the Write Mentor program.

When not writing, Marisa likes to imagine herself as a mermaid, and can often be found in the local pool...or lake...or ocean. Despite her undeniable bookworm credentials since she was knee-high to a grasshopper, the author gig took Marisa by surprise. You see, she had a secret past as a bit of a science geek during her school days. But hey, science and storytelling make a surprisingly magical concoction!

Currently, Marisa calls Woking, UK, her home sweet home, where she resides with her trusty squad, including her husband, three amazing kids, and a furry four-legged friend named Copper.

Marisa loves to hear from her readers. You can find and connect with her at the links below.

Twitter & Instagram: @MarisaNoelle77

Tiktok: @MarisaNoelle12

Website: www.MarisaNoelle.com